'Let me be the first to tell you the good news.'

Crossing one bare foot over the other, Finn leaned back with more of the insolence he'd doubtless been born with. 'Somehow I don't believe you mean *good* in the literal sense.'

'Oh, I don't know. We could learn a lot from each other, you and I.'

The true meaning of that statement lay between them, gathering momentum with every passing second. It would take time, of course. To get him to talk. To unearth his secrets. To make him crack. Thankfully Serena had all the time in the world.

'I doubt that.'

The lack of innuendo suffused her with pleasure and a heady sense of power. It seemed she was finally getting somewhere.

'Why don't you enlighten me, Miss Scott? Your excitement is palpable and I find I can barely stand the suspense.'

She deflected that sarcasm with a breezy flick of her hair off her shoulder. 'I would *love* to enlighten you, Mr St George. Me and you? We're about to be stuck like glue.'

A shadow of trepidation passed over his face before he cocked an arrogant brow. 'And the punchline is…?'

Musing that the word *babysitter* didn't quite have the right ring to it, she let her impetuous mouth stretch the truth, not really giving a stuff.

'You're looking at your new boss.'

Victoria Parker's first love was a dashing, heroic fox named Robin Hood. Then came the powerful, suave Mr Darcy, Lady Chatterley's rugged Lover—the list goes on. Thinking she must be an unfaithful sort of girl, but ever the optimist, she relentlessly pursued her Mr Literary Right, eventually found him lying between the cool, crisp sheets of a Mills & Boon® and her obsession was born.

If only real life was just as easy…

Alas, against the advice of her beloved English teacher to cultivate her writer's muse, she chased the corporate dream and acquired various uninspiring job titles *and* a flesh-and-blood hero before she surrendered to that persistent voice and penned her first Mills & Boon® romance. Turns out creating havoc for feisty heroines and devilish heroes truly *is* the best job in the world.

Victoria now lives out her own happy-ever-after in the north-east of England, with her alpha exec and their two children—a masterly charmer in the making and, apparently, the next Disney Princess. Believing sleep is highly overrated, she often writes until three a.m., ignores the housework (much to her husband's dismay) and still loves nothing more than getting cosy with a romance novel. In her spare time she enjoys dabbling with interior design, discovering far-flung destinations and getting into mischief with her rather wonderful extended family.

A recent title by the same author:

A REPUTATION TO UPHOLD
PRINCESS IN THE IRON MASK

THE WOMAN SENT
TO TAME HIM

BY
VICTORIA PARKER

Published in Great Britain 2014
by Mills & Boon, an imprint of Harlequin (UK) Limited,
Eton House, 18-24 Paradise Road, Richmond, Surrey, TW9 1SR

© 2014 Victoria Parker

ISBN: 978 0 263 24184 6

Harlequin (UK) Limited's policy is to use papers that are natural,
renewable and recyclable products and made from wood grown in
sustainable forests. The logging and manufacturing processes conform
to the legal environmental regulations of the country of origin.

Printed and bound in Great Britain
by CPI Antony Rowe, Chippenham, Wiltshire

THE WOMAN SENT
TO TAME HIM

For my Dad.
Always my anchor in the storm. I love you.

CHAPTER ONE

Monte Carlo, May

*Hold on to your hearts, ladies, because racing driver
Lothario Finn St George is back in the playground of
the rich and famous.*

*After sailing into the Port of Monaco with a bevy
of beauties only last eve, the man titled Most Beautiful in the World donned a custom-fit tux and his signature crooked smile and swaggered into the Casino
Grand with all the flair of James Bond. Armed with
his loaded arsenal of charismatic charm, the six-times
World Champion then proceeded to beguile his way
through the enamoured throng—despite the owner of
Scott Lansing advising the playboy to 'calm his wild
partying and tone down adverse publicity'.*

*Seems Michael Scott is still battling with threats
from sponsors, who are considering pulling out of over
forty million pounds' worth of support for the team.*

*True, Finn St George has always danced on the
devilish side of life, but of late he seems to be pushing
some of the more family-orientated sponsors a fraction
too far. Indeed, only last week he was pictured living
it up with not one but four women in a club in Barce-
lona—apparently variety really is the spice of his life!*

Though, with only two days to go until the Prince of

Monaco launches this year's race, we suspect Finn's wicked social life is the least of Scott Lansing's worries, because clearly our favourite racer is off his game.

While Australia was a washout, earning him third place, St George barely managed to scrape a win in Malaysia and Bahrain, leaving Scott Lansing standing neck and neck with fierce rivals Nemesis Hart. But when he crashed spectacularly in Spain last month, and failed to finish, racing enthusiasts not only dubbed him 'the death-defyer', but he slipped back several points, leaving Nemesis Hart the leader for the first time in years.

Has St George really lost his edge? Or has the tragic boating accident of last September, involving his teammate Tom Scott, affected him so severely?

Usually dominating the grid, it appears our much-loved philanderer needs to up his game and clean up his act, or Scott Lansing may just find themselves in serious financial straits. One thing is certain: while Monaco waits with bated breath for the big race tomorrow Michael Scott is sure to be pacing the floors, hoping for a miracle.

A MIRACLE…

With a flick of her wrist, Serena Scott tossed the crumpled newspaper across her father's desk. 'Well, she was wrong about one thing. You're not pacing the floors.'

On a slow spin the black and white blur landed in front of him, hitting the glass with a soft smack. Then the only sound in the luxurious office on the Scott Lansing yacht was Serena's choppy breathing and the foreboding thump of her heart.

'No pacing. Yet,' he grated, dipping his chin to lock his sharp graphite eyes on hers.

Well, now… She had the uncanny notion that after hours of musing over the true genesis of her three a.m. wake-up call she was about to discover exactly why she'd been dragged from her warm bed in London to globetrot to the Côte d'Azur. And if the suspicion snaking up her spine was anything to go by she wasn't going to like it.

'I have no idea what you're worried about,' she said, perfectly amiable as she folded her arms across the creased apple-green T shrouding her chest. 'Finn is performing to his usual sybaritic standards, if you ask me. Fraternising with God-knows-who while he parties the night away, drinks, gambles, beds a few starlets and crashes a car for the grand finale. Nothing out of the ordinary. You knew this two years ago, when you signed him.'

'Back then he wasn't this bad,' came the wry reply. 'It's not only that. He's...'

That familiar brow furrowed and Serena's followed suit. 'He's what?'

'I can't even explain it. He goes on like *nothing's* happened but it's like he's got a death wish.'

She coughed out an incredulous laugh. 'He hasn't got a death wish. He's just so supremely arrogant he thinks he's indestructible.'

'It's more than that. There's something...dark about him all of a sudden.'

Dark? A sinister shiver crept over her skin as the past scratched at her psyche, picking at the scab of a raw wound. Until she realised just *who* they were talking about.

'Maybe he's been overdoing it on the sun deck.'

'You're being deliberately obtuse,' he ground out.

Yes, well, unfortunately Finn St George brought out the worst in her—had done since the first moment she'd locked eyes with him four years ago...

Serena flung her brain into neutral before it hit reverse and kicked up the dirt on one of the most humiliating experiences of her life. Best to say lesson learned. After that, what with her engineering degree, working alongside the team's world-famous car designer in London and Finn's thirst for media scintillation—which she avoided like the bubonic plague—face-to-face contact between them had been gratifyingly rare.

Until—*just her rotten luck*—their formal 'welcome to the team' introduction, when he'd struck at every self-preservation instinct she possessed, oozing sexual gravitas, with challenge and mockery stamped all over his face. *Hateful* man. She didn't need reminding she was no *femme fatale*—especially by a Casanova as shallow as a puddle.

Add in the fact that his morals, or lack thereof, turned her stomach to ice, from the outset they'd snarled and sparked and butted heads—and that had been *before* he'd stolen the most precious thing in the world from her.

A fierce rush of grief flooded through her, drenching her bones with sorrow, and she swayed on her feet.

'Look,' her father began, tugging at the cuff of his high-neck white team shirt. 'I know you two don't really get along…'

Wow, wasn't *that* an understatement?

'But I need your help here, Serena.'

With an incredulous huff she narrowed her eyes on the whipcord figure of Michael Scott, also known as Slick Mick to the ladies and Dad when in private, or when she was feeling particularly daughterly, as he rocked back in his black leather chair.

Nearing fifty, the former racing champion reminded her of a movie icon, with his unkempt salt and pepper hair, surrounding a chiselled face even more handsome than it had been at the peak of his career. The guy was seriously good-looking. Not exactly a father figure, but they were friends of the best kind. At least they usually were.

'This is your idea of a joke, right?' It was hard to sound teasing and only mildly put out when there was such a great lump in her throat. 'Because, let me tell you, I have more of a chance to be Finn St George's worst nightmare than his supposed…*saviour.*'

The idea was ridiculous!

Visibly deflating, he shook his head tiredly. 'I know. But I find myself wondering if you have a better chance of getting through to him. Because, honestly, I'm running out of ideas. And drivers. And cars.' Up came his arm in a wave of exasperation and the pen in his hand soared over the toppling towers of paperwork. 'Did you watch that crash last month? Zero self-preservation. The guy is going to get himself killed.'

'Let him.' The words flew out of her mouth Serena-style—that was before she could think better of it or lessen the blow. One of her not-so-good traits that landed her in trouble more often than not...

'You don't mean that,' he said, with the curt ring of a reprimand.

Closing her eyes, she breathed through the maelstrom of emotions warring in her chest. No, she didn't mean that. She might not like the man, but she didn't want anything bad to happen to him. Much.

'What's more, I refuse to lose another boy in this lifetime.'

The hot air circling behind her ribs gushed past her lips and her shoulders slumped. Then, for the first time since she'd barged in here twenty minutes ago, she took a good look at Michael Scott—a real look. Her dad might be all kinds of a playboy himself, but she'd missed him terribly.

Inspecting the grey shadows beneath his eyes, Serena almost asked how he was coping with the loss of his only son. Almost asked if he'd missed *her* while she'd been gone. But Serena and her father didn't go deep. Never had, never would. So she stuffed the love and the hurt right back down, behind the invisible walls she'd designed and built with the fierce power of a youthful mind.

Yeah, she was the tough cookie in the brood. She didn't grieve from her sleeve or wail at the world for the unfairness of it all. Truly, what was the point? She was this man's daughter, raised as one of the pack. No room for mushy emotions or feminine sentimentality spilling all over the place.

So, even though she now had a Tom-sized hole in her heart, she had to deal with it like a man—get up, get busy, move on.

It was a pity that plan wasn't working out so well. Some days her heart ached so badly she was barely holding it together. *Don't be ridiculous, Serena, you can hold up the world with one hand. Snap out of it!*

'Anyway, you can't stay in London all season, fiddling with the prototype. I thought it was ready.'

'It is. We're just running through the final testing this week.'

'Good, because I need you here. The design team can finish the trials.'

I need you. Wily—that was what he was. He knew exactly what to say and when.

'No. You need me to try and control your wild boy. Problem is I have absolutely no wish to ever set eyes on him again.'

'It wasn't his fault, Serena,' he said wearily.

'So you keep saying.'

But exactly which part of Finn taking Tom to Singapore on a bender and Finn coming back first-class on his twenty-million-pound jet whilst her brother returned in a box wasn't his fault? Which part of Finn taking him out on a boat when Tom couldn't swim and subsequently drowned wasn't his fault? He hadn't even had the decency to attend the funeral!

But she didn't bother to rehash old arguments that only led her down the rocky road to nowhere.

'So you want me to…what? *Forgive* him? Not a chance in hell. Make him feel better? I don't. So why should he?'

'Because this team is going down. Do you really want that?'

She let loose a sigh. 'You know I don't.' Team Scott Lansing was her family. Her entire life. A colourful, vibrant rabble of friends and adoptive uncles and she'd missed them all. But the entire scene just brought back too many memories she was ill-equipped to handle right now.

'So think of the bigger picture. Read my lips when I say, for the final time, it wasn't Finn's fault. It was an accident. Let it go. You are doing no one any favours quibbling about it—least of all me.'

He pinched the bridge of his nose as if to stem one of his killer migraines and guilt fisted her heart.

He was suffering. They were all suffering. In silence. *Let it go...*

But why was it every time they spoke of that tragic day, when the phone had shrilled ominously through their trailer, she was slapped with the perfidious feeling she was being kept in the dark? And she *loathed* the dark.

It didn't matter how many times she asked her father to elucidate he was forever cutting her off.

'Tom wouldn't want to see you like this,' he said, irritation inching his volume a decibel higher. 'Blaming Finn. Doing your moonlit flit routine. Holing up in London. Burying your head in work. You've done all you can at base—now it's time to get back in the field. Quit running and stop hiding.'

'I haven't been hiding!'

He snorted in disbelief.

Okay, maybe she'd been hiding. Licking her wounds was best attempted in peace, as far as she was concerned. But honestly...? How far was solitude getting her on the heart-healing scale?

Serena's heavy lids shuttered. God, she was tired.

She'd lost her brother, her best friend, and she kept forgetting she was supposed to carry on regardless. This was tough love and she'd been reared on it. Admittedly the vast majority of the time she'd appreciated Michael Scott's particular method of parentage. You needed skin as thick as cowhide to trail the world for ten months of the year in the company of men. Not the best way to raise two children, but she'd genuinely loved her life. Honest.

If she'd often stared at other children with their mothers, wondering what it would be like to have one of her own, to live in a normal house and walk to an actual brick-built, other-children-present school every morning, she'd just reminded herself that her life was exciting. And if she'd prayed for a mum all those years ago when her adolescence had been shattered, leaving her broken and torn, she'd comforted herself that she had Tom. Tom had been her rock.

But now he was gone. Nothing was exciting any more and there was no one to hold her hand in the dead of night when the shadows loomed. *You don't need your hand held. You're stronger than that. Snap out of it!*

She swallowed around the lump in her throat, forcing the overwhelming knot of grief to plunge into her chest. Buried so deep her stomach ached.

'*If* what you say is true and there *is* a problem,' she said dubiously, 'how can *I* possibly help?'

'Get him to take an interest in the prototype or work on your latest designs... I don't know—just get him to focus on something other than women or the bottom of a bottle.'

Impossible.

'*I'm* a woman.'

'Only in the technical sense.'

'Gee, thanks.' As if she needed reminding.

Then again, the last thing she wanted was to be like one of Finn's regulars. They were the skirt to Serena's jeans. The buxom bombshells to Serena's boyish figure. The strappy sandals to Serena's biker boots. The super-soft, twice-conditioned spiralling blonde locks to Serena's wild mane of a hue so bizarre it defied all colour charts.

Which was wonderful. Inordinately satisfying. Exactly the way she liked it.

'The last thing he needs is another bedmate,' he muttered wryly. 'He needs a kick up the backside. A challenge. And, let's face it, you two create enough spark to fire a twin-stroke. Therefore I am asking—no, you know what…? I am *telling* you to help. You're on my payroll. You move back in here and you chip in.'

Tough love.

Then his graphite gaze turned speculative. Calculating. An expression she didn't care for that nailed her to the wall.

'Or you can kiss the Silverstone launch of your proto-type goodbye.'

A gasp of air hit the back of her throat. 'You wouldn't dare.'

'Wouldn't I?'

Yeah, he probably would. He didn't believe the racing car she'd designed would be anything special and she'd do anything to prove him wrong.

That prototype was her baby. Three years of hard work. Her and Tom's inspiration. Launching at Silverstone had been their dream. The only tangible thing she had left of him.

'Low, Dad,' she choked out. '*Really* low.'

Averting his eyes, he scrubbed a palm over his face. 'More like desperate.'

Serena sighed. Nailed. Every. Time.

'Fine. I'll try…something.'

Unease began to hammer at her heart—she had no idea how to handle the man. None.

'But I know Finn will make it up. He had a slow start last year. The sponsors will forgive and forget once he starts playing to his fans. Monaco is in the bag. He always wins here. What happened in qualifying sessions today? He's in pole position, right?'

Her father's expression turned thunderous—one that boded only ill. 'He screwed the engine.'

He blew the engine? 'So he's at the back tomorrow? In one of the slowest and hardest circuits in the world?'

'Yep.'

Pop! Up came a vision in her mind's eye—the scene she'd

bypassed as she'd hauled her motorbike along the harbour—and her stomach fired, anger swirling like a tornado. Sparking, ready to ignite.

Raising her arm, she pointed one trembling finger in the general direction of Finn's floating brothel. 'And he's along there, in that…that yacht of his. Engaging in some kind of… drunken debauched sex-fest to celebrate his latest cock-up?'

One weary hitch of those broad shoulders was all it took to light the fireball raging in the pit of her stomach.

'What in the blue blazes is he *doing*? Doesn't he care at all? In fact, don't answer that. I already know.'

The man cared for no one but himself! *And this was a newsflash?* Obligation and decency had clearly been disowned in that gene pool.

'I've had it with him.'

Bullet-like, Serena shot out through the door, her biker boots a clomp-clomp on the polished wooden floors as she raced through the galley. 'I'm gonna kill him. With my bare hands.'

'Serena! Watch your temper. I need him.'

Yeah, well, she needed her brother back—and that was about as impossible as keeping her mitts off Finn St George's pretty-boy face. She'd had enough of that man messing with her family. Her team. Her life. Her brother was dead, the championship was heading for the toilet, and her dad was aging by the second as Finn continued to yank at his fraying tether!

How selfish could one man be?

Well, she was stopping it all. She was taking control.

Right now.

CHAPTER TWO

Serena ducked and dived around the loved-up couples milling on the harbour, her sole focus on the *Extasea*, rising from the water, formidable and majestic.

Even moored among some of the finest vessels in the world, Finn's super-yacht was in a class of her own—a one-hundred-and-sixty-foot, three-decker palace—reminding Serena of the resplendent seven-star hotels he favoured in Dubai and certainly more regal ocean liner than bordello.

Still, opulence aside, she had the acumen to know that appearances were deceptive, and the fact that she'd been lowered to this chafed her pride raw. But there was no backing out now. She was going to say her piece and he was going to listen.

The bravado felt wonderful. Freeing. Cleansing. She should have done this months ago, she realised—had it out with him instead of letting everyone sweep her under the carpet like some bothersome gnat, as if her feelings were of no importance. Her grief had been so all-consuming that she'd allowed it to happen. Well, not any more.

Closer to the yacht now, she felt the balmy air cling to her skin and the thud of her boots become drenched by the evocative beat of sultry music. As she marched up the gangway the splash of water from the hot tub on the sun deck followed by intimate squeals of sexual delight made her trip over her size fives.

Flailing, she gripped the rail on both sides. Then a tidal wave of apprehension crashed over her and she stood soaked with a keen embarrassment. She was about as comfortable with this scene as she would be treading water in the company of killer sharks.

You don't belong here, Serena. Surrounded by sex and women who exuded femininity. *Don't think about it. Just get in there, find Finn, and make him clean the decks himself!*

Hovering a few feet from the top, she inhaled a deep wave of saltwater air to reel back her bravado.

In every direction—whether it was left, towards the luxurious seating area abounding with plush gold chairs, or right, towards the outer dining suites—there were bodies, bodies and more bodies. Wearing as little clothing as possible.

She shivered, chilly just looking at them.

One step further and still no one seemed to notice the impromptu arrival of an uninvited guest. No ravaging lips ceased to kiss. No fervent hands slowed their bold caresses of sun-kissed flesh. No flutes of champagne paused on their way to open mouths and the laughter rolled on in barks of joyful humour that only served to remind her of the last time *she'd* laughed—which made a scream itch to peal up her throat.

Why should Finn and his entourage be laughing when she was still unable to cry? Unable to shed one solitary tear? *Because boys don't cry...*

Indignation launched her the final few feet and out of nowhere a sinister-looking figure loomed and grabbed her wrist in a manacled grip.

'Ow!' Pain shot up her arm and she flipped her hand in an attempt to dislodge the hold—even as she was flung back in time and any lingering panic was ramped up into bone-shattering fear. 'Get off me!'

Except the more she struggled, the tighter the hold became—until the knife-edge of terror scored her heart and her vision swam in the blackest waters...

A rough yet familiar voice shattered the obsidian glaze. 'Hey, let her go. She's okay.'

Mr Manacle released her so fast she stumbled backwards. Her only conscious thought was that she was taking up self-defence classes again. Pronto.

Righting her footing, she glanced at the owner of that masculine rumble.

'Thanks,' she murmured, her voice disgustingly fragile as she rubbed at her wrist to ease the throb of muscle and friction burn.

'You okay, Serena?'

Vision clearing, she focused on the handsome, boyish face of one uneasy chocolate-haired Jake Morgan. Scott Lansing protégé and an apparent star in the making. She'd never watched him drive. For some reason he always got a bit tongue-tied around her, and the fact that he was Tom's replacement gave her heart a pang every time she looked at him. *Not his fault, Serena. Let it go.*

'Peachy. Since when does Finn have security?'

'Had them on and off all season. Mainly for parties when there's a big crowd.'

Translation: when he needed to fend off gatecrashing bombshells.

'Where *is* your dissolute host?' she asked, somewhat surly and unable to care. She was shaking so hard she had to cross her arms over her chest to stop her bones rattling.

'Not sure.' Jake's Adam's apple bobbed and his eyes jerked to a door leading to what she guessed was the main salon. 'I haven't seen him for a while.'

Oh, wonderful. He was covering for Finn. 'Forget it. I'll find him myself.'

The sensation of copious eyes poring over her wild mane and crumpled clothing made her flesh crawl and she had to fight the instinct to race across the polished deck. Ironically, the door to the devil's lair suddenly seemed very appealing and she slipped inside with a bizarre sense of relief.

The lavishness of the place was staggering, and way too gold-filigree-and-fussy for her. She might have a DNA glitch but it didn't even suit Finn. Granted, he'd purchased the mega-yacht from some billionaire, but at least a year had passed since.

After ten minutes of being creeped out by cherub wall sconces she was standing in a corridor surrounded by more doors. It was all like a bad dream...

Moaning, purring, steamy and impassioned noises drifted from the room at the far end of the panelled hallway, licking her stomach into a slow, laborious roll.

Pound-pound went her heart as she edged further towards the sounds, her gaze locked on the source as if drawn by some powerful magnetic force.

Her hand to the handle now, a wisp of a thought passed through her brain: did she *really* want to catch Finn the notorious womaniser *in flagrante* with his recent squeeze? She had enough nightmares to contend with at the best of times. Except...she could hardly roam around here all night, could she? If he was in a drunken stupor she only had sixteen hours to clean him up, and she was *not* leaving this place without some answers!

Astounded at what she was about to do, she pressed her ear up against the door panel in an effort to decipher voices.

Rustle went the sheets and *creak* went the muffled bounce of springs, as if bodies were interlocked and undulating in an amorous embrace. Cries of rapturous passion bloomed in the air and her blood flushed hotly, madly, deeply, in an odd concoction of mortification, inquisitiveness and warmth.

Jeepers, what was *wrong* with her?

Focus.

Ignoring the anxious thump in her chest warning that exposure was imminent, she leaned further in and relished the cool brush of wood against her fevered flesh.

The woman, whoever she was, was clearly glorifying in what was being done to her. No subdued cries or awkward silences while she wished it were over. Just murmurs of encouragement in a deep velvet voice that made the damp softness between Serena's legs tighten.

Not Finn. She would recognise that seductive rasp of perfect Etonian English laced with the smattering of an American drawl any day. A distinct flavour from the time he spent in the off season, presenting a hugely popular car show in the States.

Not that she *liked* his testosterone-and-sex-drenched tone—not at all.

Edgy, she licked her arid lips and told herself to back away before she was nabbed. So why couldn't she move? Why did she strive to imagine what was happening behind this door? Wonder how, precisely, Mr Velvet Voice adored his lover's body for her to reach such hedonistic heights that she became paralysed, unable to do anything but scream in wanton pleasure and abandon—?

'Has she come yet?'

A voice, richly amused and lathered with sin, curled around her nape.

A squeak burst from her throat.

Her head shot upright.

Boom! Her heart vaulted from her chest and she pivoted clumsily, then spread herself against the door panel like strawberry jam on toast.

One look…

Oh. My. God. *No!*

Squeezing her eyes shut she began to pray. *This is not happening. Not again. I am not the unluckiest woman alive!*

'Good evening, Miss Seraphina Scott. Come to join the party?' he asked, with such unholy glee that she was fuelled with the urge to smack her head off the door. 'There's always room for one more.'

'When…' Oh, great—she couldn't even breathe. And her heart—God, her heart was still on the floor. 'When hell freezes.'

She wanted out of here. *Now.* Except the idea that she was

acting like a pansy made her root her feet to the floor like pesky weeds and she prised her eyes wide. Only to decide being a sissy wasn't so bad.

Leaning insolently against the polished panels, no more than two feet away, Finn St George smouldered like a banked fire and the heat spiralling through her veins burst into flames, seared through her blood. All she could think was that she must have done something atrocious in another life to deserve this.

After what he'd done, had it truly been too much to hope his mere presence would have stopped affecting her?

She hated him. *Hated* him! He hadn't changed one iota. Still the most debauched, moral-less creature on two legs. And clearly he intended to go on as if he *hadn't* taken a crowbar to her life and smashed it to smithereens. What had her father said? *'He goes on like nothing's happened...'*

Over her dead body.

Seraphina. No one was allowed to call her that. No one!

'This isn't a social call, I assure you,' she said, proud of her don't-mess-with-me voice as she restrained the urge to shiver before him. 'Any other time it would take an apocalypse to get me into this den of iniquity.'

His mouth—the very one that had been known to cause swooning and fever-pitch hysteria—kicked up into a crooked smile and one solitary indentation kissed his cheek. 'And yet here you are.'

Here she was. It was a pity, that for a moment, she couldn't remember why. All she could think was that that mouth of his was a loaded weapon.

'I do seem to find you in the most...*deliciously* compromising situations, Seraphina.' His prurient grin made his extraordinary eyes gleam in the dim light. 'Listening at doors? Bad, bad girl. I ought to take you over my knee.'

Thanking her lucky stars that she wasn't prone to blushing like a girl—because, let's face it, she'd never *been* one, and the fact that this man made her feel like one was probably the greatest insult on earth—she weighed up the intelligence of answering that symphony of innuendo. Meanwhile she returned his visual full-body inspection just as blatantly. Why he insisted on going through this rigmarole every time they met was a mystery. With one arching golden brow he arrogantly put her in her place—ensuring she understood that she was a duck among swans.

Unluckily for him intimidation didn't work on her. Not any more.

As she soaked up every inch of him she decided she didn't understand the man's appeal.

Obviously there had to be some basis for his being named the world's greatest lover, an erotic legend in the racing world. But, come on, plenty of men must be good in bed—right? Plenty had sexy dimples in lean jaws. Plenty had a mouth made for sin, lips that moved sensually and invitingly and downright suggestively, and eyes the colour of—

Ohhh, who was she kidding?

Finn St George was flat-out, drop-dead *insanely* gorgeous—an abundance of angelic male beauty.

Thick dirty-blond hair; cut short at the back and longer at the front to fall in a tousled tumble over his brow, gave him a sexy, roguish air. And that face...

Not only did he defy nature, he literally bent the laws of physics with his intriguingly wicked mouth and that downright depraved gleam in his cerulean eyes. Eyes that had catapulted him into the hearts and fantasies of women the world over.

Between his leading-man looks and his celebrated body—currently dressed in low-slung board shorts and an unbuttoned crisp white linen shirt, showcasing his magnificent torso—he was mouth-watering, picture-perfect in every single way.

It was a good thing she knew how well a polished chassis could hide an engine riddled with innumerable flaws.

'What do you think you're playing at, Lothario? Don't you

think drinking and partying the night away before a race is
dangerous, even for you?'

'I have to find *some* way to work off the residual adrenaline rush from the qualifying session, Seraphina. Unless
you're offering to relieve some of my more…physical ten-
sions.'

Her lower abdomen clenched in reaction to that catastrophically sensual drawl, and as if he could sense it his
lips twitched.

'I'd be quite happy to knock you out—would that help?'

There it was again. That smile. A dangerous and destruc-
tive weapon known to bring women to their knees. And the
fact that it turned her own to hot rubber made her madder
still. 'Then again,' she sniped, 'we wouldn't want to mar that
pretty-boy face, would we?'

A trick of the light, maybe, but she'd swear he flinched,
paled…before something dark and malevolent tightened the
hard lines of his body until he positively seethed.

Whoa…

Her mind screaming, *Danger! Danger! Run!*, she backed
up a step and nudged the door. She wanted to snarl and bite
at him. It was as if her body knew he was the enemy and
she was gearing up for a fight. The fight she'd once been
incapable of.

Not any more.

Her blunt nails dug into her palms, but in the next breath
he pursed that delectable mouth in suppressed amusement,
as if it had all been some huge joke, and the change in him
was so swift, so absolute, she floundered.

'There's something dark about him all of a sudden.' Or
she could be hallucinating from an overdose of his pheromones.

'If you don't mind,' he drawled, 'I'd appreciate it if we
kept my face out of it. After all, I wouldn't want to distress
the ladies with some unsightly bruising.'

'Like you need any more ladies! Looks to me like you've had your fair share already this evening.'

He looked well-sexed, to be sure. Hair damp, with his glorious fresh water-mint scent flirting with her senses, she guessed he'd just stepped from beneath the assault of a shower.

'On the contrary, I was just about to indulge in a good workout.'

Disgust drove her tone wild. 'Yes, well, bedding the latest starlet or pit-lane queen is one thing—partying the night away before racing on the most dangerous circuit on the calendar is downright risky and inappropriate!'

He gave an elaborate sigh. 'Where is the fun in being *appropriate*? Even the word sounds dull, don't you agree?'

'No, I don't—and nor do our sponsors.' She rubbed her brow to pacify its exasperated throb. 'I swear to God, if you don't start pulling through for this team I will make you wish you'd never been born.'

'You know, I believe you would.'

'Good.'

He brushed the pad of his thumb from the corner of his mouth down over the soft flesh of his bottom lip. 'So if you haven't come to indulge in some heavy petting why are you here, beautiful?'

His voice, disturbingly low and smooth as cognac, was so potent she swayed, nigh on intoxicated.

For an infinitesimal moment his cerulean-blue eyes held hers and a riot of sensations tumbled down the length of her spine. Pooled. Pulled. Primal and magnetic. And she hated it. Hated it!

Beautiful?

'Don't mock me, Finn. I'm not in the mood for your games. I want this place cleared and you sober. How *dare* you party it up and put the team at risk while everyone sits around feeling sorry for your little soul?'

'You know as well as I do that sympathy is wasted on me.

Especially when there is a profusion of far more...*enjoyable* sensations to be experienced at my hands.'

Ugh.

Temper rising, implosion imminent, she felt her breasts begin to heave. 'For someone who blew up an engine this morning— and, hey, this is a *wild* idea—how about you start thinking of how to salvage the situation instead of screwing around? Have you been drinking? You could get banned from the race alto- gether!'

With a shake of his head he tsked at her. 'No drinking.'

'You swear?'

One blunt finger scraped over his honed left pec. 'Cross my heart.'

Time stilled as she walked headlong into another wall of grief and memories slammed into every corner of her mind. The games of two children. One voice: *'Cross my heart.'* The other: *'Hope to die.'*

There it was. The elephant in the room.

Tom.

Cold. Suddenly she was so very, very cold. Only want- ing to leave. To get as far away from this man as she could before the emotion she'd balled up in her chest for months punched free and she screamed and railed and lashed out in a burst of feminine pique.

She'd tell her dad he was barking up the wrong tree. No way could she work with Finn. She felt unhinged, her body vibrating with conflicting emotions, all of them revving, striving for pole position. And that was nothing compared to the hot whirlpool of desire swirling like a dark storm inside of her. How was that even possible? How was that even fair?

Life isn't fair, Serena. You know that. But what doesn't kill you makes you stronger. Makes your heart beat harder and your will indestructible.

So before she left she was getting the answers she wanted if it was the last thing she did.

* * *

In all the times over the last eight months when Finn had imagined coming face-to-face with Seraphina Scott, he'd never once envisaged the tough, prickly and somewhat prissy tomboy with her ear smashed against a door panel, listening for the orgasmic finale sure to come.

How very...*intriguing.*

It had certainly made up his mind on how to handle her impromptu arrival. With one look his heart had paused and he'd stared at the sweet, subtle curve of her waist, battling with innumerable choices.

Apologise? Not here, not now. Wrong place, wrong time. The risk that his defences would splinter equalled the prospect that she wouldn't believe him.

Wrap her tight in his arms because for a fleeting moment he'd sensed a keen vulnerability in her? Far too risky. If he buried his face in that heavenly fall of fire he might never come up to breathe again.

Act the polite English gentleman? Despite popular opinion he was more than capable of executing that particular role. He could be anyone or anything any woman wanted, as long as it wasn't himself. The problem was that kind of outlandish behaviour would only make her suspicious and no doubt she'd hang around.

He might be responsible for the words *delectable, fickle* and *playboy* appearing in the dictionary, but he was far from stupid. Soon she'd start asking questions about her brother's death, and he had to ensure they never came to pass those gloriously full raspberry lips. Lips he'd become riveted upon. Lips he'd do anything to smother and crush. To make love to with every pent-up breath in his taut body until she yielded beneath his command.

Never.

So in the end he'd settled for their habitual sparring. The usual back and forth banter that was sure to spark her every nerve and induce the usual colourful dazzling firework display. Make her hate him even more. Followed by her departure, of course.

While a vast proportion of him had rebelled at the notion, some minuscule sensible part had won out. After all, if there were fairness and justice in the world *he* would be the man six feet under and not an innocent kid who'd always looked at him as if he were some kind of hero.

What a joke.

But death eluded him. No matter how many of life's obstacles he faced, and no matter how many cars he crashed. He was Finn St George—dashing, death-defying racing driver extraordinaire. Death took the good and left the bad to fester—he'd seen that time and time again. Not that he deserved any kind of peace. When it finally came and he met his maker he doubted he'd hear the sweet song of angels or bask in the pearly glow of heaven. No. What waited for him was far darker, far hotter. Far more suited to the true him.

Was he worried? Hell, no. Rather, he looked forward to heading down into fire and brimstone. It couldn't be much worse than what he'd lived with all day, every day, for the last eight months.

Ah, great. There he went again. Becoming ridiculously maudlin. Entirely too tedious. A crime in itself when faced with the delectable Miss Seraphina Scott, who never failed to coerce a rush of blood to speed past his ears.

Clink. The door behind her opened and a bikini-clad blonde shimmied past, trailing one French-tipped talon down Finn's bare forearm. A soap opera star, if he remembered correctly, and a welcome distraction that twisted his torso as he watched her saunter down the hall with a practised sway of her voluptuous hips.

What he couldn't quite discern was why his eyes were on one thing while his mind, his entire body, was attuned to another, riding another wavelength—one set on Seraphina's ultra-high frequency.

Typical. Because—come on—if there was ever a more

desirable time to regain some kind of sexual enthusiasm for his usual coterie of fanatics it was the precipitous return of Miss Scott.

'One of yours, I presume?'

Derision drizzled over that strawberry and cream voice making every word a tart, sweet bite.

'I don't believe I've had the pleasure.' Turning back to her, he licked his decadent mouth in a blatant taunt. 'Yet...'

Shunning her sneer of scorn, Finn gave an unconcerned shrug. Women had been flinging themselves in his direction since he'd hit puberty. What kind of man would he be to deny their every sensual wish? Anyway, he loved women—in all their soft, scented glory. Almost as much as he loved cars. It was a shame the current state of his healing body continued to deny him full access.

Not that he was concerned. It would fix itself. He just had to make sure he was a million miles away from *this* woman when it happened.

'Do you think you could refrain from thinking with your second head for one solitary minute?'

He pretended to think about that and in the silence of the hallway almost heard himself grin. 'I *could*. If you made it worth my while.'

Three. Two. One. *Snap*.

'You're a selfish bastard—you know that? Anyone else would try and focus on the good of the team after we lost Tom. Or should I say after *you* took Tom from us?'

Strike one. Straight to his heart.

'But not the consummate indestructible Finn St George. No, *no*. You think only of yourself and what slice of havoc you can cause next. If it isn't women, it's barely being able to keep a car horizontal.'

'While horizontal is one of my *preferred* positions, I admit it doesn't always work out that way.'

Grimacing, she moaned as if in pain. 'Don't you take

anything seriously? You crashed a multimillion-pound car last month. One I doubt will ever see the light of day again.'

He scrubbed a palm over a jaw that was in desperate need of a shave. 'That was unfortunate,' he drawled. 'I agree.'

'Is everything a joke to you?'

'Not in the least. I just find it tedious to focus on the depressing side of life. I'm more a cup half full kind of guy.'

'Unfortunately that cup of yours is going to run on vapour if you don't start winning some races.'

Yeah, well, he was having a teeny-tiny problem getting any shut-eye, thanks to the flashbacks visiting him far too often for his peace of mind. And, while his driving had always controlled the restless predator that lived and breathed inside him, of late that wildness had overtaken all else. Until even behind the wheel he felt outside of his own body. Detached. His famed control obliterated. Even as he wiped his mind he could still feel the tight scarred skin of his back rubbing against his driving suit—and then... *Hello, flashback.*

Luckily his body was healing. The memories would pass and he had all season to make it up to Michael Scott. Thirteen races to land the championship. Piece of cake.

'Don't worry about a thing, baby, the team is in safe hands with me.'

It was, of course, entirely possible Michael didn't think him capable of pulling them out of the quagmire. Hence this visit from Little Miss Spitfire.

'Now, why does that fail to ease my mind? Oh, yes—because these days, unlike Midas, everything you touch meets a rather gruelling end.'

Strike two, sending his heart crashing into the well of his stomach even as he managed to hide his wince with another kick of his lips. 'You need to trust me, baby.'

She snorted. 'When sheep fly and pigs bleat. I'm pretty sure the first step to trust is actually liking the person.'

He let his debauched mouth fire into a full-blown grin.

Finally—someone who loathed him instead of walking on

eggshells and spouting blatant lies to his face that it wasn't his fault. Michael Scott had a tendency to do just that. But Finn wasn't blind to the turmoil in the other man's eyes. The reality was his boss had a team to run and they were locked in a multimillion-pound contract, so Mick had no choice but to keep him around until the end of the season. The fact the man had to look at him every day left a bitter taste in Finn's mouth. Mick was a good guy. He deserved better.

After years of driving with the best teams in the world, constantly restless, his itchy feet begging to move on, he'd hoped he could settle with Scott Lansing for a while. It was more family than moneymaking machine, and respect ran both ways. Little chance of that now, but he'd win this season if it were the last thing he did.

As long as this woman stayed out of his way.

'Also, do me a favour, would you? Quit the *baby* thing. It suggests an intimacy I would rather die than pursue.'

Then again, he couldn't see close proximity being a problem, because—*oh, yeah*—she wanted to stamp on his foot good and proper. He could see it in those incredible eyes. Eyes that were a sensual feast of impossibly long dark lashes acting like a decadent frame around a mesmerising blend of the calmest grey with striations of yellow-gold as if to forewarn that there was no black and white with this woman—only mystifying shades of the unknown. Ensuring he was continually intrigued by her. Bewitched by her secrets. Yet at the same time they promised peace, true tranquillity—a stark, stunning contrast to that hair.

Her hair...

A shudder ripped through his body just from looking at it, inciting pure want to move through his bloodstream like a narcotic. Because that spectacular mane of fire told him she'd been burned and lived to tell the tale. A survivor.

Shameful, reprehensible; his eyes took a long, leisurely stroll down her lithe little body, soaking up her quirky ensemble.

Clumpy biker boots which, more often than not, made him instantly hard. Skin-tight denims and an apple-green T with the words 'It's All Good Under the Hood' stroking across her perfect C's.

Ohhh, yeah, she was delicious. Lickable. Biteable.

She leaned towards a serious tomboy bent and after multiple seasons of being faced with silicone inflation, Botoxed lips and an abundance of flesh on show, looking at Seraphina Scott was dangerous to say the least. Intrigue gave way to intoxication every time. Unfortunately he'd just have to suffer the side effects—because she was the one woman he could never, *ever* touch.

Not only was she the boss's daughter, and not only did that tough outer shell conceal an uncontrollable fiery response that lured the predator inside him to prowl to the surface and claw down those walls, but he'd also made a promise to her brother—and he'd stand by it even if it killed him...

'If I don't get out of this alive, Finn, promise me something?'

'Don't talk like that, kid. I'll get us out of here.'

'Whatever you do, don't tell Serena about this place. She's been through enough. She'll go looking for blood. You have to keep her safe. Promise me...'

His lungs drew up tight, crowding his chest until he could barely breathe. He would keep her safe. By getting her away from him.

Shuttering his eyes for a brief spell, he blocked her mesmeric pull. He'd dreaded this moment for months, he realised. Knowing she would come out fighting even as grief oozed from her very pores.

Where once she'd been a little bit curvy, now she was a little bit too thin. A stunning force of anger and sadness, beautiful and desolate. As if heartbreak had pulled the life force out of her and every morsel was tasteless.

Finn had done that to her.

Tom Scott...

Guilt lay like crude oil in the base of his stomach and every time he looked at her it churned violently, threatening to catch fire, making him ache. *Ache.* God, did she make him ache. Make the mourning suffocate his soul. As if it wasn't enough that the kid was still his constant companion even in death.

He didn't want her here. In fact he wanted her as far away from him as he could get her. Which begged the question: why was she back?

She who now eyed him expectantly and for the life of him he couldn't remember what she'd said.

Shifting gears, he asked, 'How's London?'

'Cold.'

'How's work?'

'Great. Thank you for asking,' she said, with such a guileless expression he didn't even see the freight train barrelling down the hallway. 'Why didn't you come to Tom's funeral? He worshipped you.'

His stomach gave a sickening twist.

'Sick.' He needed off this topic. *Right. Now.* 'How's the prototype?'

'Spectacular. Sick how?'

'Boring story. Is it finished?'

Say no.

Fuming at his attempt at derailing the conversation, she breathed slow and deep. 'Maybe. Did you know he couldn't swim?'

Crap. 'No.' *Not at the time.* 'Are you staying?'

'Possibly.'

Dammit. This was getting too close for comfort. 'I think you could do with more time off,' he said. 'Take a holiday.'

Suspicion narrowed her glare. 'Is that right?'

'Sure. How about a nice sojourn round the Caribbean? All that sun, sea and sex would do you good. Loosen you up a little.'

She raised one delicate dark brow. 'Why, Finn, I didn't know you cared.'

'There's a lot you don't know about me.'

'Funny, I was just thinking the exact same thing.'

Now he remembered why he couldn't stand the woman. 'Anyway, I was saying. A holiday is just what you need.'

'Are you saying I don't look so good?'

'Well, now you come to mention it you *are* a little on the thin side.' True, most women would consider that a compliment, but Miss Scott wasn't like other women.

As predicted, she prickled like a porcupine. But at least she wasn't musing about funerals and swimming any more.

'Trading insults, Finn? I wouldn't advise it. You've buried yourself in so much dirt over the years I'll always come out on top.'

A growl ripped up his throat. 'Mmm... You on top. Now, *that* is something I would love to see,' he said, sending his voice into a silken lazy caress, frankly astonished at how much effort he was expending to keep this up. For the first time in history one of their sparring sessions was stealing great chunks of his sanity.

'Liar. Furthermore, I'm not one of your fans or bits of fluff, so do me a favour and keep those blues above neck level. If you're trying to intimidate me you'll have to do a better job than feigning interest and eying me up.'

'But it's so much fun watching you prickle.'

'Some of us have a deeper meaning in life than having fun, and fickle playboys don't bring out the best in me.'

'Oh, I'm not so sure about that.'

Fired up, she was a whole lot of beautiful. Which he supposed was why he'd always tumbled into the thrust and parry of verbal swords with her. Sparks truly did fly when he was duelling with Miss Scott.

Now she was breathing in short, aggravated bursts, her breasts pushing against her rumpled T, and his fingers itched to climb beneath the hem. She'd be *sooo* lusciously soft, one hundred per cent organic and berry-like delicious against his tongue as he sucked her nipple between his lips…

Heat scrambled up his legs, heading straight for his groin… Until she crossed her arms over her chest, jerking his attention to the red blotches that marred her delicate wrist.

'What are those marks?' Closing the gap, he leaned in for a better look. 'What *is* that?'

'That is a gift from your security detail, keeping the hordes at bay.'

Hordes at bay? 'Let me see.'

'No!' Tucking her hands tighter into the creases of her underarms, she regarded him as if he were ten kinds of crazy.

'Come on. Stop being a girl. It doesn't suit you.'

'You know, that's the first truth you've uttered since I got here.'

As he gently tugged her hand free his knuckles brushed over her soft breast. *Holy…* More heat raced south, pleasure and pain moving through him at full throttle.

Oh, man, the last thing he needed was his first hard-on in almost a year to be for this woman. It was an inconceivable prospect that was swiftly overtaken by the dark bruising marring her wrist, and his insides shook with anger as he remembered the sight and sensation of torn wrists, shredded skin, blood dripping from shackles.

'Finn?' she breathed. 'What are you…?'

With deliberate and infinite care he brushed the backs of his fingers down one side of her forearm and up the other. 'I…' *I'm sorry he hurt you. I'll make him pay. I swear it.*

'Finn?'

Tilting her head, she frowned. Cutely. The action softened the often harsh yet no less cataclysmic impact of her beauty.

Seraphina Scott wasn't pretty in the normal sense of the word. She was no delicate English rose. No, no. She was a wild flower. Tempestuous and striking. Made in technicolour. Hardy, tough. Weathering every storm, only to survive more beautiful than ever before.

And she was clearly waiting for him to expand. Trying to work him out.

Such a small thing, that softening. It made her appear vulnerable. From nowhere more words sped through his brain. *I'm sorry...I'm sorry. So very sorry I took Tom away from you. I would do anything. Anything to bring him back.*

How he wished he could tell everyone the truth. Let the world know what had truly gone down in Singapore. But with an ongoing investigation and a sense that he'd meet his adversary again one day it was impossible. Business hadn't been settled. Too many men roamed free. So if there was to be a next time he was going in alone.

As if she knew the direction of his thoughts, she shaped her lips for speech—no doubt to ask more questions he would never answer, couldn't even bear to hear. Tension throbbed like a living force, so heavy he could taste it, feel the weight of it pressing on his shoulders.

What was it going to take for him to get rid of her? He didn't want Serena near him. Hell, he felt dangerous at the best of times. Around her he felt positively deadly. The need to charge upstairs and throttle the security guy's neck roiled inside him, toxic and deadly, and surely he had enough blood on his hands.

Speaking of hands... For some reason he couldn't let hers go. She was trembling. It couldn't possibly be him. Finn required a large hit of G-force to feel moved.

Holding her wrist in the cradle of his palm, he reached up with his other hand to touch the wild mass of her hair. Hair the deepest darkest red, reminding him of ripe black cherries.

How long had he resisted the temptation of her? It felt like a thousand years.

Almost there and her eyes caught the movement, flared before she jerked backwards.

'Finn. Let go of me. Right now.'

Distantly he heard the words, the quiver in her command,

and knew they held no heat. Control slipped from his grasp and he fingered the stray lock tumbling over her shoulder.

Pure silk. Hot enough to singe. Fire burning on a dangerous scale.

Ignoring her sharp gasp, he corkscrewed the thick wave and tugged. Hard. Being rough. Too rough. But that was what she did to him. Severed his control. Fed his wildness. Even as the thought of hurting her fisted his heart.

'Fiiiinn...' she warned, as her chest rose and fell in rapid, mesmerising waves.

Familiarity rattled her. Always had. After the last time he'd touched her, however innocently, she'd avoided him for four years. Clever girl, she was.

Not once had he seen her embrace her father and he'd never noticed her with a lover. It couldn't possibly be through lack of interest. Whether they would admit it or not, every guy on every team wanted a piece of her, Jake Morgan in particular carried a huge crush. But they always kept their distance. Prewarned? he wondered. Or did none of them have the courage to take her on?

There was a story there. One he'd pay any price to discover. One he would never know.

And that, he realised, was his answer. Or at least he told himself it was.

The charm he'd been born with, the charismatic beauty he'd wielded like a golden gun since he'd been old enough to deduce the fact that it got him out of many a sticky situation, would be the one thing—the only thing—to drive her away. Back to London. Out of sight. Out of mind. Free from the claws of temptation.

It wasn't as if he could do any harm. Despite every word that fell from her delectable pout, she felt the same exquisite thrill of attraction he did. Hated it just as much as he did.

Decision made. It was bye-bye, Miss Seraphina Scott.

May the gods forgive him for what he was about to do.

He unleashed his desire and went in for the kill.

CHAPTER THREE

LIKE A RABBIT caught in the headlights, Serena's heart seized, and her eyes flared as the world's most beautiful man brushed the back of his knuckles up the curve of her jawline.

Weakness spread through her limbs and she started to shake as if she'd been injected with something deadly. And when he skimmed the super-sensitive skin beneath her ear and sank his fingers into the fall of her hair to anchor her head in place dark spots danced behind her eyes.

'Don't you dare,' she barked. Or at least she intended to. Bizarrely, it came out as more of a panting plea.

'You should know better than to challenge me, Miss Scott. Especially in that gorgeous husky voice of yours.'

'Honestly, Finn, will you stop that for just one minute?'

'What?'

'The lies.' She loathed them. Not only did they torment the girl beneath, desperate to believe him, they also whispered of a long-ago web of deceit, a dark betrayal that haunted her soul.

'I'm not lying, baby,' he murmured.

The crackle of energy sizzling between them turned sharper—a sense of anticipation much like the coiled silence before the boom of thunder.

Surely he wasn't going to...? He'd be crazy even to contemplate...

His body came up flush against hers—all hard lines,

latent strength and super-hot heat—sending shock waves straight through her. Then his free hand splayed over her waist, swept around the small of her back and tugged her closer still, until every inch of their bodies—her soft curves and his hard-muscled form—were fused together with need and sweat and fire.

Need? No, no, no. *Impossible.*

'*Wow*, you really do have a death wish, don't you? You're on a collision course for total bodily destruction here, Finn.' Bending her knee, she aimed it to jerk upwards into his groin. Or maybe from this angle she could hook her foot around his ankle and send him off balance...

Kiss.

His lips pressed against the corner of her mouth, then brushed across the seam of her lips.

Ohhh, not good—not good at all. Especially when he moaned low in his throat and started to...well, to nuzzle his way over her cheek, then flick the tip of her nose with his to coerce her head back. And whatever had taken over her body answered his every command.

A heated ache bloomed between her legs, and when he nibbled on her lips to prise them apart the electric touch of his tongue was like a shot of high-octane fuel surging through her.

Don't respond. Don't you dare kiss him back.

'No...' she breathed, hating him. Hating herself even more for wanting. Flailing...

Serena reached up to push him away but ended up grabbing fistfuls of his shirt, holding on for dear life, powerless to sever the warm, moist crush of his mouth against hers as he moved with a consummate and inexorable seductive ease to find the perfect slick fit for their mouths.

Oh, my life. His kiss was slow and lazy, not meant to enflame but to enrapture, and before she knew it she was whirling in the epicentre of the fiercest storm, bringing her own force of nature into play.

She shivered and arched into him. *Never* had she felt anything like it. That warm, damp place between her legs throbbed together with her heartbeat and she wriggled closer, pushing her breasts into his chest to relieve the heavy, needy ache.

Tender and fiercely intimate, he didn't take her will, he invited. He didn't invade her body, he lured. He didn't punish her for her internal struggle, he tempted and teased with an amorous touch.

The pure sensual pleasure of it all was enthralling, making her feel feminine in a way she'd never dreamed possible. A way no man had made her feel before.

He deepened the kiss—the languorous thrust of his tongue a velvet lash of tormenting pleasure. It poured through her veins, heated her bones and weakened her limbs. It blasted all thought from her head until her most basic sexual instincts screamed for him to be inside her. Instincts she'd never known she possessed...

There were reasons for that, of course. She—

Whether it was the rush of unwanted memories or the gentle touch of his hand deviating on a feral bent to roughly fist and yank at the hem of her T, she wasn't sure, but—*oh, God*—he might as well have dunked her in an ice bath.

Emotion was a burning ball at the base of her ribs—embarrassment, humiliation and a heart-rending vulnerability that brought tears to her eyes. *No! No tears.* But all of it, all at once, was so overpowering that her mind began to shrill.

Flattening her palms, she shoved at his chest. Finn instantly let go and took a large pace backwards, that awesome chest heaving as he held both hands in the air in a show of surrender.

Intelligent guy.

The walls of the hallway began to close in on her as she gulped hot air. 'What the blazes are you doing?'

Taut silence pulsated off every surface as Finn blinked

dazedly and scrubbed his palms down his face, playing the role of slightly rattled, wholly astonished, guiltless gent! He belonged on the stage—he really did.

He gave his head a good shake. 'Seeing if your lips taste as good as they look.'

'What?'

He must think her dense. A fool. She was so far removed from his usual entourage she might as well derive from another planet, and for months he'd poked and prodded at her blatant lack of femininity. Now he expected her to believe his impetuous come-on was legitimate?

He was messing with her and she knew it.

And how could she have forgotten Tom? The part this man had played in her brother's death?

Guilt climbed into her chest and sat behind her ribs like a heavy weight. It crushed her lungs, making her breath shallow, her voice high-pitched. 'Answer me, Finn! What was that about?'

His lips parting to speak, he faltered yet again.

Why did she feel as if he wanted to tell her something? Something vital. Something she desperately wanted to hear. Nothing but the truth.

Rightly or wrongly—more than the next race, more than his success or the victory of Team Scott Lansing—the promise of that truth was the only thing tempting her to hover in his orbit.

Hold on…

'Are you trying to get rid of me? Is that your game?'

Wow, it seemed the heights of her humiliation knew no bounds.

Finn blinked several times in rapid succession and with every flutter of those ridiculously gorgeous thick lashes his expression smoothed into unreadable impassivity, until once more she was looking at Lothario.

'Is it working?' he drawled.

'Yes!'

'Good,' he said, those legendary dimples winking at her. 'Then you'll be pleased to know the door is that way.'

With a swift finger towards said exit, he pushed open a panel to her left. One he strolled through before it closed behind him, leaving her standing there, jaw slack, twitching in temper. The nerve of the man!

Fury grounded her flight instinct.

He wanted rid of her? He could go to the devil! This was *her* family, *her* life, and she was staying put. Her team was in trouble because of him and he needed to pay his dues. Not forgetting the fact he was hiding something and she wanted to know *exactly* what. Maybe then she could start to repair her broken heart and let Tom go. Move on. Find some peace. Remember what it was like to enjoy life—although she often wondered if she ever had.

Two steps forward, she pushed at the panel of what appeared to be a secret doorway. If it hadn't budged an inch and then rebounded back with a slam she would have thought it locked. Was he leaning on the other side, trying to regulate his breathing like she was? *Don't be a gullible fool, Serena.* He'd be grinning like the feckless charmer he was, delighted that he'd got the better of her.

The second time she put all her weight behind the oak, pushed and stumbled into a room, tripping over her feet with as much elegance as a battering ram.

A zillion things hit her at once—mainly gratitude for the fact that her ungainly entrance was witnessed only by Finn's back as he swaggered towards the bed and the sheer extravagance of the room.

'Wow.'

Infinite shades of midnight blue, the decor was a pulse-revving epitome of dark sensuality and masculine drama, and about the only thing on this floating bordello that fitted the man himself. As if, after purchasing the mega-yacht, Finn had only stamped ownership on this one room.

'Did you run out of money before the renovations were

complete?' she asked, tongue in cheek, knowing full well he was one of the highest earning sportsmen in the world.

For a beat he paused at the side of the bed. 'Let's just say I decided the yacht didn't suit. She's on the market.'

'Now, that *is* a shame.' If he restored the rest of the yacht in the same vein it promised to be spectacular.

'Do you like my bedroom, Seraphina?'

His voice was a pleasured, suggestive moan as he flung himself atop a gargantuan carved bed covered in black silk sheets and propped his back against a huge mound of textured pillows.

'I love it,' she said, unable to hide her awe and trying her hardest to look anywhere but at him. 'Present company excluded.'

Black wood furniture lined walls of the deepest red, with the spaces in between splashed with priceless evocative art to create a picture of virile potency and sophisticated class. It was visually breathtaking. Until the intimacy of the dim lighting set her right back on edge.

Searching the darkened shadows behind her, she cleared her throat, 'Lights?' she said, and hoped she didn't sound as jittery as she felt.

Bending at the waist, he leaned sideways to press a button on the tall glass nightstand and the opaque ceiling flickered for one, two, three beats of her thundering heart before the night sky shone down upon the room, ablaze with a million twinkling stars.

The sheer magnificence pulled her eyes wide. 'Seriously?'

He plucked a large red apple from the colourful mound of ripe delicacies toppling from a crystal bowl, then straightened up and raised one of his heart-stopping smiles.

Just like that her unease drifted, melted like a chilled snowflake on a new spring breeze.

Moonlight frosted his body, from the open white linen draping his sides to the wide bronzed strip of naked torso in between, taking his powerful beauty from angelic to super-natural. Otherworldly. Dazzling, magical and utterly surreal.

And she forgot all about not looking at him, suddenly entranced.

He tucked one hand beneath his head, tossed the glistening red fruit up into the air with the other and his honed six-pack flexed and bunched—the sight bringing a mist of perspiration to her skin.

'So. Come back for more, Miss Scott?'

His sinful rasp shattered the spell he wove so effortlessly and she gave herself a good shake. The man was *lethal*.

'I have heard my mouth is highly addictive.'

Serena raised a brow and hoped she looked suitably unimpressed. She had no desire to stroke his ego or any other part of him ever again. 'Such a...tempting offer, Mr St George, but I think I'll pass. Your reputation has been highly exaggerated.'

Apple to his lips, he sank his teeth into the crisp flesh with a loud *crunch* and she dredged the taste of tart flesh from her memory banks, making her mouth water.

'Ah. Must have been the champagne, then.'

'What must have been the champagne?' she murmured, distracted by the rhythmic working of his lean jaw. It truly was *not* good form to be so sexy even when eating. 'The champagne, incidentally, that I did not drink.'

'The weakening of your knees,' he drawled, with a wicked satisfaction that rolled over her in hot waves before he let loose an irrepressible grin that seared her nerves.

One day... She thought. One day she was going to wipe that smirk off his face once and for all. The thought that today was as good a day as any made her let loose a smile of her very own.

Strangely, he froze mid-bite. As if her smile affected him just as much as his did her. The mere notion that he had the power to make her believe such a thing made her temper spike.

'Speaking of knees—I'm going to bring you down on yours, pretty boy.'

A curious tension drew the magnificent lines of his body taut, precisely as before, and she racked her brain to figure out the trigger. All she could think was that there was more to this man than met the eye.

In the next instant he relaxed. 'I do hope that's a promise, Seraphina. I'd be more than happy to oblige.'

Blowing out a pent-up breath, she deliberated over how long she could ride this roller coaster of emotion with Finn at the helm before she plunged to her doom.

Especially when he licked his lips hungrily and dropped his feral blue eyes to the seam of her jeans, to the zipper leading down to the tight curve of her femininity. From nowhere an image of Finn on his knees before her as she stood bathed in moonlight slammed into her mind's eye. *Oh, God.*

Ribbons of heat spun in her veins, moving through her blood in an erotic dance. Her skin was suddenly super-sensitive, and her nipples chafed seductively against the soft fabric of her plain white bra. The shockingly carnal expression on his face made her wonder if he'd visualised the very same.

As if. He's just trying to distract you again and you're letting him!

She stiffened her spine and ordered her voice to sweet. 'Oh, I'm so glad. In that case, let me be the first to tell you the good news.'

Crossing one bare foot over the other, he leaned back with more of the insolence he'd doubtless been born with. 'Somehow I don't believe you mean *good* in the literal sense.'

'Oh, I don't know. We could learn a lot from each other, you and I.'

The true meaning of that statement lay between them, gathering momentum with every passing second. It would take time, of course. To get him to talk. To unearth his secrets. To make him crack. Thankfully she had all the time in the world.

Another flash of perfect teeth sinking into white flesh. Another lazy crunch. Another sexy swallow gliding down his throat. 'I doubt that.'

The lack of innuendo suffused her with pleasure and a heady sense of power. It seemed she was finally getting somewhere.

'Why don't you enlighten me, Miss Scott? Your excitement is palpable and I find I can barely stand the suspense.'

She deflected that sarcasm with a breezy flick of her hair off her shoulder. 'I would *love* to enlighten you, Mr St. George. Me and you? We're about to be stuck like glue.'

A shadow of trepidation passed over his face before he cocked an arrogant brow. 'And the punchline is…?'

Musing that the word *babysitter* didn't quite have the right ring to it, she let her impetuous mouth stretch the truth, not really giving a stuff.

'You're looking at your new boss.'

CHAPTER FOUR

FANS DESCENDED ON Monaco in their droves and celebrities flocked to the world's most glamorous sporting event of the year for the exhilarating rush of lethal speed and intoxicating danger. So it didn't bode well that Finn stood in the shade of the Scott Lansing garage, his temples thudding with a messy blend of sleep-deprivation and toxic emotional clatter.

He had to get it together. Get that little minx out of his head.

Hauling in air, he rolled his neck, searching for the equilibrium he needed, knowing full well the smallest of errors in these narrow streets were fatal. Overtaking almost impossible... And didn't that just make him smile? Feel infinitely better as a fuel injection of hazardous adrenaline shot through his bloodstream?

Monaco was hands down his favourite circuit in the world: the greatest challenge on the racing calendar. It never failed to feed his wildness and remind him that life was for living. A master at shutting off fear and anxiety, he was a man who existed in the moment. Life was too short.

Seize the day.

Finn closed his eyes, tried to block the memory those words always evoked. But of late, since he'd touched hell itself, his past refused to stay buried.

Thirteen years old and he'd watched his Glamma—the woman who'd been a second mother to him—die a slow, agonising death. *'Glamma, because I'm far too young and viva-cious to be Gran,'* the award-winning actress would declare.

Even when she'd been sick and he'd sworn his heart was breaking—*'Carpe diem, Finn, seize the day,'* she'd say the-atrically, with a glint in her eye that had never failed to make him smile. *'That's better. Always remember: frown and you frown alone, smile and the whole world smiles with you.'*

Yeah, he remembered. How could he possibly forget a leg-end who had been far too young and vibrant for her passage to the heavens. Then, when the cancer had seeped into the next generation and his mother's time had come—spreading more grief and heartache through his family, much like the stain of her disease, destroying her beauty, her vitality, her life—he'd vowed to live every day as if it were his last. And, considering the way Finn had handled her demise, he owed his mother nothing less.

His heart achingly heavy, he left the technical chatter of the engineers behind and stepped towards the slash of sun-light cutting across the tarmac, shoving the pain and guilt back down inside him.

Enthusiasts spilled over balconies and crammed rooftops as far as the eye could reach. The grandstands were chock-full, the area where the die-hard fans had camped from the night before roared with impatience, and huge TV screens placed for optimal viewing flickered to life. It was a scene that usually enthralled him, excited his blood. And it would. Any second now. It had to.

His attention veered to the starting grid, cluttered with pit crew and paddock girls flaunting their wares, and then muttered a curse when not one of them managed to catch his eye. No, no. The only woman who monopolised his thoughts was his ruby red-headed *boss*!

Talk about a simple meeting of mouths backfiring with stunning ferocity. Instead of pushing her away, he'd stoked her curiosity—and how the devil he'd managed to step away, not to devour her, he'd never know.

Good thing he was an expert at disposing of the opposite sex. He'd just have to try harder, wouldn't he? With a touch of St George luck, Serena would make herself scarce today.

He snorted in self-irritation. Now he was lying to himself. He might *need* her at the far ends of the earth but he *wanted* her here, didn't he? Why was that? She was sarcastic, she had a sharp, spiky temper, and she was beautiful but not *that* beautiful—he'd dated catwalk models, for God's sake. *Yeah, and found them dull as dishwater.* And on top of all that just looking at her made him feel guilty.

Self-castigation, he decided. Penitence dictating that he had to make himself suffer by hanging around with a woman who wanted him dead.

He rubbed at his temple and thrust the same hand through his damp hair. Where on earth was she? Some boss she was turning out to be—

He chuffed out a breath. Boss? Doubtful. Babysitter, more like. She had spunk—he'd give her that.

Suddenly the crowd erupted and in the nick of time he realised he'd stepped into the blazing sunlight. Up came his arm in the customary St George wave as the pandemonium reached fever pitch. On cue, he whipped out his legendary smile, even as the movement of his torso pulled his driver's suit to chafe against his scarred back and black despair churned in his stomach with a sickening revolt.

Keep it together, Finn.

'There you are. Playing to your adoring audience, I see.'

Whoa—instantaneous body meltdown. The woman held more firepower than the midday sun.

'How nice of you to turn up, Miss Scott,' he drawled, keeping his focus on the crowd for a few seconds longer. Let her think he was inflating his ego—the worse she thought of him the better—but Finn knew how far his fans had travelled, the huge expense. He'd spoken to hundreds of them over time after all.

'I would've been here sooner if I hadn't detoured to that

floating bordello of yours, looking for you. I much prefer today's security man, by the way. New shift?'

He shrugged. Made it indolent, couldn't-care-less. 'Probably.'

Alternatively Finn might have shown the other man the error of his ways the minute Miss Scott had stepped off his... What did she call it? Oh, yes—his *floating bordello*. Naturally Finn would have used his most amiable, charming voice. The one he used to express how tedious a situation had become, how boredom had set in. The very one which ensured that people made the terrible mistake of underestimating him. Shame, that.

If that *had* happened the man in question might have been escorted from the premises in a not so dignified manner, with a reference that not so subtly informed the world that he'd never work in the industry again. Together with the unequivocal, downright irrefutable notion that to meet Finn in a dark alley any time soon would be a very, *very* bad idea.

Would he tell her any of this highly amusing tale? God, no.

Why ruin a perfectly good reputation as a callous, nogood heartbreaker when it was security money couldn't buy. Women had more sense than to expect more than he could give, so there was no fear of broken hearts or letting anyone down. What you saw was what you got.

And Miss Scott was no exception. Not now. Not ever.

Rousing a nonchalance he really didn't feel, he glanced to where she stood beside him; hands stuffed into the back pockets of her skin-tight jeans, the action up-tilting her perky breasts, and his pulse thrashed against his cuffs.

Then his heart turned over, roaring to life as he checked out her white T-shirt, embellished with a woman clad in a slinky black catsuit and the words 'This Kitty Has Claws' stroking across her perfect C's.

How beautifully apt.

'Lucky kitty,' he drawled, stretching the word as if it had six syllables. 'Can I stroke it?'

A shiver rustled over her sweet body and his smile warmed, became bona fide, as she slicked her lips with moisture. 'If you need all ten fingers to drive I wouldn't advise it.'

'I love it when you get all mean and tough. It turns me on.' It was that survivor air about her. Did strange things to him.

'Forgive me if I don't take that as a compliment. Seems to me that anything with the necessary appendage flicks *your* switch.'

'You'd be amazed at how discerning my sexual palate is, Miss Scott.'

Very true, that. After a few disturbing front-page splashes in his misbegotten youth he'd vowed to take more care in his liaisons. Absolute honesty with women who read from the same manual. Short, sweet interludes. No emotions. No commitment. Ever.

The mere word *relationship* caused a grave distress to his respiratory rate.

Not only had he started to see himself as some kind of bad luck charm—a grim reaper for those he cared for—but he was also inherently selfish. Driving was his entire life. Women were simply the spice that flavoured it.

Existing in the moment wasn't exactly conducive to family ties when he travelled endlessly, partied hard, and there was every possibility there would be no tomorrow.

She snorted. 'Discerning? Yeah, right.' And she brought those incredible grey eyes his way, arching one brow derisively. 'Let's take this conversation in a safer and more honest direction, shall we? Where's your helmet and gloves?'

'Not sure. Be a good little girl and go get them for me, would you?' he drawled, his amusement now wholly legit.

She puckered those luscious lips at him and a layer of sweat dampened his nape.

'Don't push it, Finn. I promise you, you don't want to get on the wrong side of me today.'

He dipped his head closer to her ear and relished the way her breathing hitched. 'I would *love* to get on any side of you, Seraphina. Especially now I've tasted that delicious mouth of yours.'

Easing back, he licked his lips to taunt her with the memory. It certainly wasn't to try and remember her unique flavour—that tart strawberry bite sparking his taste buds to life. Incredible.

'In your dreams.'

'Always,' he said, knowing she wouldn't believe him. Odd that it made him feel safe enough to drop his guard, tell her the unvarnished truth—which was a danger in itself.

With an elaborate sigh she stormed into the shadows of the garage, her voice trailing off to a murmur as she spoke to the mechanics and engineers. *Yes, go—get as far away from me as you can.*

From the corner of his eye he noticed a news crew focusing on him with the ferocity of an eagle spotting its prey and his chest grew tight. *No chance.*

Feigning ignorance, he ducked his head and strode back into the shade. Where he ran smack-bang into a helmet.

'Here,' Serena said, slapping a pair of gloves in his other hand.

A shaft of shock rendered him speechless. She used to bring Tom his helmet and gloves. She used to murmur something too. At one time Finn had tried to eavesdrop, but he'd quickly decided he was being ridiculous and didn't care what she'd said.

Then she'd always run to meet her brother after the finish, whether he'd won or not. She'd run out and hug him warmly, affectionately, with admiration in her smile and trust in her heart.

Instead of the usual envy the memory evoked, he battled with another surge of guilt that she couldn't run to Tom any longer. Then called himself fifty kinds of fool for toying with the idea that she could run to him if she needed to. *As if.*

'Hey, are you with me?' She clicked her fingers in front of his face. 'You're phasing out, there. Something I should be worried about?'

Out came his signature smile. 'You worried about me, baby?'

'No. I'm worried about the multimillion-pound car you're likely to crash to lose the championship! Did you get some sleep?'

Strangely enough, the couple of hours he'd managed had been demon-free, with his new boss the star of the show. Which was typical of him—wanting something he could never have just to make the challenge more interesting. The win more gratifying. Because, let's face it, while he fed off the rush of success, it never seemed to be enough. He was always restless. Always wanting something elusive, out of reach.

So, no, he did not trust himself around her. 'I did catch a few hours, thank you. It's amazing what the presence of a sexy spitfire can achieve.'

Her delicate jaw dropped as she grimaced. 'You mean after I left you actually…?'

Finn shook his head in disbelief. She thought he was talking about someone else.

Why was it that she'd grown up surrounded by men and yet had no conception of her unique brand of sexuality? It was as if she lacked self-confidence. If so, he wished she'd start believing him. Wished he could show her what she did to him.

Too dangerous, Finn. Just get in the car, win the race, show her you're a fixed man and get her back off to London out of harm's way.

The pep talk didn't work a jot. And, come on, she might fancy the pants off him but it wasn't as if she would ever answer to this overwhelming burn of desire. One, she was an intelligent little thing and she had more sense. And, two, she hated his guts.

'After *you*—sexy spitfire that *you* are—left, I slept. Alone.'

Her mouth a pensive moue, she simply stared at him.

Finn watched the soft shimmer of daylight dance through the shadows to cast the lustre of her skin with a golden radiance, enriching the heavy swathe of her hair until the strands glittered with the brilliance of rubies. A shudder pinballed off every vertebra in his spine.

'Why do you do that?' she asked, more than a little frustrated.

'What?' Shudder?

'Say things you don't mean.'

'Who says I don't mean them?'

She gave a little huff. 'Past experience. You've always delighted in ensuring I know you see me as nothing more than a tomboy.'

'Tomboys can't be sexy?' She was the sexiest woman he'd ever laid eyes on. And that was before she wrapped that incredible body in leathers to straddle her motorbike or—*give him mercy*—put on a driver's suit. Then it was, *Hello, hard-on; bye-bye sanity.*

He had no right to slide his gaze over her body in a slow, seductive caress, trying to remember the sight.

The boots moulded to her calves shuffled uneasily. 'Stop it!'

'You don't like it.'

Statement. Fact.

'No. I don't.'

Why? Because the extraordinary chemistry bothered her? Or because she was experiencing it with the man who'd stolen her happiness?

While the reminder punched him in the heart, it didn't stop him from saying, 'So why don't you take the compliment for what it is, baby? The truth.'

Crossing her arms over her chest, she hiked her chin up. 'But I don't want practised compliments from your repertoire. They mean nothing to me. I merely want you to do your job.'

Knife to his gut. Fully deserved. For the first time in his life he rued his reputation.

The smooth skin of her brow nipped and he realised his emotions must be seeping through the cracks in his façade. He schooled his expression with ruthless speed as his guts twisted in anger. One false move with this woman and he'd be finished.

'Look, Finn....' She sighed softly. 'I know you want to win this race and you've held the title for four years, but positioned at the back...? It's too risky an endeavour for even *you* to try and take the lead. I don't think anyone has ever done it before.'

If that wasn't a red rag to a bull he didn't know what was. He was also *pretty* sure being careful wasn't the name of the game.

'So just try and get a decent finish and come back here with the car in one piece, okay?'

For a second he thought he saw fear blanch her flawless complexion. Fear for him. And something warm and heavenly unfurled in his guts. Until he realised she merely wanted the car back in one piece. *Idiot.*

'Yes, boss,' he said, with a cheeky salute as he sealed up the front of his suit.

'Good,' she said, and the word belied the cynicism in her eyes. 'Now, get your backside in that car and let's see some St George magic.'

Walk away. Finn. Walk away and stop playing with her like this. You cannot have her!

'You think I'm magic?'

'I think you display a certain amount of talent on the track, yes.'

'My talents—

'If what is about to come about of your mouth has any reference to bedroom antics I will knock your block off.'

Finn cocked a mocking brow. 'I wasn't about to say any-thing of the sort. My, my—haven't we got a dirty mind?'

'Liar,' she growled, long and low, like a little tigress, and he almost lost his footing as he backed out of the garage.

How did the woman do it? Make him feel alive for the first time in months. Make his smile feel mischievous and his body raw and sexual when no other woman could.

Narrowing her glare, she lifted one finger and shook it. 'I don't like that smile, Finn. I really don't. Whatever you're thinking, whatever stunt you're about to pull...'

The scorching rays hit his nape, the crowds chanted his name and he unloaded his charismatic arsenal and licked his lips. 'Trust me, baby.' Slanting her a wink that made her blink, he veered towards the Scott Lansing race car. 'Trust me.'

Finn was sure she muttered something like, *Not in this millennia*, and he smiled ruefully. If she had any sense she'd remember that.

Inhaling long and deep, he infused his mind with the ad-dictive scents of hot rubber and potent fumes that stroked the air—as addictive and scintillating as the warm, delicious redhead he'd left back at the garage.

Within ten minutes he was packed tight behind the wheel, the circuit a dribble of glistening molasses ahead of him, pushing his foot to the floor until the groans and grunts of the powerful machine electrified his flesh. Oh, yeah, he was a predator, with a thirst for the high-octane side of life, the thrill of the chase. One goal—to win.

Pole position. Middle or back. Dangerous or not. Didn't matter to him.

This race was his.

Trust him. *Trust him?*

'What the blazes is he doing?' It was, quite literally, like waiting for the inevitable car crash.

One of the engineers whistled through his teeth. 'Look at that guy go. Phenomenal, isn't he?'

'Crazy, more like,' she muttered. Zero self-preservation. *Zero!*

More than once she heard the pit-lane channel go silent and probably wouldn't have thought anything of it—*if* she hadn't noticed him do that thing last night and this morning. Almost phasing out as some kind of darkness haunted his gaze. It was disturbing since he was renowned for his awesome ability to concentrate with such focus that nothing else existed but his car hugging the tarmac.

A battalion of bugs crawled up her spine and she glanced back at the shaded screen hanging in the garage.

'Grand Hotel Hairpin. Just ahead of him. Holy Toledo! It's a pile-up.'

Her heart careening into cardiac arrest, she held her breath, waiting for the iconic red Scott Lansing car to clear the haze of dust and debris. *Come on, come on. Stuff the car. Don't you dare kill yourself. I will never forgive you.*

Serena wondered at that. Decided it was because she hadn't managed to coax the truth about Tom's death out of him yet. Tom, who should be here. Racing in this race. Doing what he'd loved best.

A fist of sorrow gripped her heart. Too young. He'd been just too young to die. And despite everything Finn was too young to be chasing death too.

She had to swallow in order to speak. 'Where is Jake?' With a bit of luck *he* had more sense.

'Still holding fifth.'

A cackle of relieved laughter hit her eardrum as Finn's car flew past the devastation to take third place.

'I don't believe it,' she said, breathless and more than a bit dizzy.

'I do.' Her dad stood alongside her now, his attention fixed on the same screen. 'Whatever you said to him has obviously worked, Serena. What *did* you say?'

'That I was his new boss.'

Michael Scott's head whipped round with comical speed. *'What?'*

'Worked, hasn't it?' she said, knowing full well that her impulsive mouth had nothing to do with it.

Finn danced to his own tune, had his own agenda front and foremost. Moreover, just watching him race like this—with the ultimate skill and talent—made her even more certain there was more to his crashes and sporadic losses than met the eye. But for some reason today he was *mostly* focused.

'He's taking second place with one lap to go! It's gonna be tight, though.'

She snorted. 'He doesn't want to lose the Monaco title.' Then she squeezed her eyes shut as he almost rammed into the Nemesis Hart driver, swerved to avoid a crash and clipped his front wing off instead.

'Whoa—there goes the car coming back in one piece.'

Stomach turning over, she shoved her hands into her back pockets to watch the last minute on screen.

Heck's teeth, he was going to do it...

Admiration and awe prised their way through the hate locked in her chest. The man was *amazing.*

'Half a second. Unbelievable!' someone yelled.

A warm shower of relief rained down from her nape and her entire body went lax.

The crowd erupted with a tremendous roar and chanted his name: *'Fi-in Fi-in Fi-in.'* Every mechanic and engineer ran out into the scorching rays and Michael Scott—who hadn't hugged her since she was fourteen years old, when she'd been broken and torn and his face had been etched with fury and pain—turned round, picked her up and spun her around the floor.

She imagined it was how a ballerina felt—spinning, twirling, dancing on air. Her beauty delicate, feminine. Nothing like *her.*

Before she even had a chance to wrap her arms around his neck, to bask in this inconceivable show of affection, to actually *feel* his love, he abruptly let go and jogged into the pit lane.

Swaying on her feet, she swallowed hard—told herself for the millionth time in her life not to be upset. That she mustn't be angry with him for not wanting to be close to her. It was just the way he was. He only knew how to deal with boys.

'*Come on, Serena, get a grip, get busy, move on,*' he'd say. '*Boys don't cry.*'

Okay, then. Get busy. Move on.

Except alone now, with the dark shadows creeping over her skin like poison ivy, she felt...lost. Grappling with the annoying sense that she was forgetting something.

Oh.

This was the part where she ran out to Tom.

Cupping her hand, she covered her mouth, gritted her teeth and tensed her midriff to stop the sob threatening to rip past her throat. *No. No!*

She should never have come back here. Should have stayed away—

Footsteps bounded from the pit lane and she sucked great, humongous lungfuls of air through her nose, then blew out quick breaths. Over and over.

It was a good job too, because Finn strode into the shadows—and the intense magnetism he exuded was a tangible, vibrant combination of devil-may-care and decadent sin.

Blond hair now dark with sweat tumbled over his brow and he wore an indecipherable expression on his over-warm face, almost as if he knew exactly what she'd been thinking. *Impossible.*

Bolstering her reserves, she stood tall as he drew near and threw his arms wide.

'What did you think, baby?'

'I think that by the end of the season I'll be on a whole

lot of medication. Good God, you're a liability.' A very expensive, scorching hot, stunning liability.

'So you don't wanna hang around with me any more?' He clapped a hand over his left pec. 'I think my heart's broken.'

'Come on, Finn, you and I both know you don't have one. You take direction from another body part entirely.'

Standing there, smouldering with testosterone, he sneaked his tongue out to moisten his lips. When it came, his voice was a low groan. 'You think about my body parts?'

That was it. Later she'd have no idea how she could veer from abject misery to munching on the inside of her cheek to stifle a snort of laughter. He was incorrigible. She hated him. *Hated* him!

'I think about many of your body parts. Your neck, especially—the very one I'd like to wrap my hands around.'

She reminded herself that to be turned on by that cocksure smile was a gross dereliction of self-preservation.

'Did you need something?' she asked, thoroughly confused. 'You've left your fans wailing for your return.'

'No, I just wanted...' He lifted his hand and scratched the side of his jaw in an uneasy, somewhat boyish manner.

'What?' she murmured, distracted by a small scar she'd never noticed before—a thin white slash scoring his hairline. How on earth had he got that?

'I wanted you to say how awesome I am.'

'Don't be silly. You can barely fit your head through the open cockpit as it is. Keep dreaming.'

'Oh, don't worry. I will,' he drawled suggestively. And just like that she was transported back to his yacht, his kiss. Then came the heat, curling low in her abdomen, licking her insides, making her shiver.

Honestly, she was certifiable. Without a doubt.

Much as earlier, he began to back out of the garage, taking his dizzying pheromones with him, and within a nanosecond fury overtook her. For the playful banter. For the way she'd allowed him to affect her so utterly.

'By the way, I want to speak to you tonight,' she said sharply.

Before he hit the bright light his feet froze mid-step. 'Saying goodbye already?'

Tilting her head, Serena frowned. 'Now, why would I do that?'

'I won the race. I'll charm the sponsors at dinner. Disaster averted.'

That was why he was so focused on winning? To get rid of her? Surely not. His need to win overruled all else. Unless what he was hiding was of far more importance.

Her heart flapping like a bird's wings against a cage, she said, 'I'm not going anywhere, Finn. I promise you that.'

Gazes locked, they engaged in some sort of battle of wills—one she had no intention of losing. She was here to stay.

'Unfortunately, Miss Scott, I have a date this evening. With my good friend Black Jack. Unless you'd care to join us…?'

'*The Casino?* I wouldn't be seen dead there.'

And the smirk on his face told her he knew it!

'Then I guess you'll just have to catch me some other time, beautiful.'

Not if she could help it. The man had to get dressed on that den of iniquity, so she'd just have to corner him before he stepped foot on the harbour. There was no way on this earth she was going up to that swanky Casino, where the dress code pronounced that all women had to dress as if they were for sale. Not for love nor money. She didn't even own a dress, for heaven's sake.

Nope. She'd just have to catch him first.

CHAPTER FIVE

FINN DIDN'T WASTE any time calling in a favour and landing a suite at the most exclusive Casino in town—where all the glitz and glamour that made the city famous came together in a fairy-tale fantasyland of opulence and high-flyers—and ordering a tuxedo from one of the exclusive concessions in the marble and bronze foyer.

Strict dress code aside, at times he luxuriated in his debonair façade. Playing Casanova was generally more interesting than being himself. Also, as it turned out, his penthouse here had evolved into a necessity. Not only did he need somewhere to sleep with no lingering residue of the demons haunting him in the dead of night, but a gratifyingly quick sale had gone through that very afternoon. One of the members of a minor royal family reviving his Swiss bank account very nicely.

The fact he was Seraphina-free for the evening was also an added boon.

The plan was, he'd grab a couple of girls, lavish money on a few gaming tables, dance until the wee hours and then sleep. Great plan. The fact that he lacked enthusiasm…? Not so great.

Her fault. It's all her fault.

Had he actually stormed into the garage to check on her? According to his memory banks, yes, he had.

Since when had he left the hullabaloo of the roaring crowd for a woman? Never before in his life!

Do not panic—it's the guilt.

Knowing she missed her brother and veiled the ache with her beautiful bravado was killing him. The pain that lurked behind those incredible grey eyes was a fist to his gut. Her strength was formidable, but he couldn't help wondering what it cost her. Of late, holding his own façade in place came at an extortionate price, but the alternative fall out would be catastrophic. As soon as he opened the door to his emotional vault the contents of Pandora's box would be unleashed and all hell would break loose.

Now, sitting in the prestigious lounge known as the throbbing heart of the Casino, he palmed a tall glass of tequila and raised it to his lips, hopeful that the sharp kick and bite would burn the dull edges off his dark mood. For some reason the suave, elegant cut of his suit wasn't working tonight. He felt dangerous enough to burst out of his skin.

The sensation of black eyes staring into his soul reminded him of dark, agonising days and he downed the liquor—his first drink in a week—and it slid down his throat, trailing a blaze of fire to his gut.

Gradually the muted *whoosh* of spinning roulette wheels, the mumble of inane chatter and the evocative beat from a small band filtered through his mind.

The singer was a stunning blend of French beauty and passionate sultry vocals, and when he felt her eyes slither over him in blatant invitation the crystal in his fist cracked with a soft clink. What was he *doing* here? He'd sell his soul to be someone else for one day, one night—

Between one heartbeat and the next the hair on his nape tingled, shifting his pulse into gear.

Easing his totalled glass onto the low-slung mahogany table, he glanced covertly around the room—from the impressive plaster of Paris inlays and priceless art to each and every table in between. By the time he reached the archway leading to the main gambling hall every cell in his body was on red alert and his heart had roared to life.

It was the kind of stupefying feeling he'd used to get on the starting grid. The very one he'd lost what felt like aeons ago, leaving a dull imitation in its place.

Now the cause of that incredible sensation shoved heat through his veins as he caught a flash of ruby-red hair flowing across the foyer.

Within seconds he was on his feet. What *was* Miss Spitfire doing in here? Looking for him? She was a determined little thing.

In the main lobby he glanced left, towards the wide entryway—seeing the line of supercars curling around the fountain beyond—and then right, to fall beneath her spell as she disappeared around a darkened corner.

By the time he caught up she was facing a door, her hand in mid-air—

'You've come to the Casino to use the bathroom, Seraphina? Do you have a problem with the plumbing on your father's yacht?'

She froze, palm flat against the hardwood panel, and Finn watched her decadent long lashes flutter downwards to whisper over her satiny cheeks. No make-up, he mused, and her natural beauty was really quite breathtaking.

With a swift inhale she spun on her feet and then crossed her arms over her knee-length black coat. She arched one delicate brow. 'When a girl needs to go, a girl needs to go.'

'How right you are.' He needed to be rid of her just as badly. Because she was angry—no, she was furious—and he wanted to kiss that mulish line right off her lips.

'You could have told me you'd sold your bordello *before* I stormed the place looking for you.'

Ah.

'I would have if I'd known you were coming to visit, baby. You know how much I look forward to our little…assignations.' He felt a smile tug at his lips. Stretching wider as her gaze loitered over his attire and a shiver racked her svelte frame.

'Am I doing it for you tonight, Miss Scott?' he asked, his voice a decadent purr.

She grimaced as if she were in pain. 'If by "it" you mean making me regret the moment I ever laid eyes on you, then, yes, strangely enough you are.'

Aw, man, she was delicious. 'How do you feel about dinner?' It was a horrendous idea, but he suddenly had the urge to feed her. Fill out those over-slight curves.

'You mean *together*?'

'That's a bit forward, don't you think? But, yes, okay. I accept.'

Mouth agape, she slowly shook her head, clearly questioning his sanity. Oddly enough, that made two of them. 'Did you attend some school specialising in becoming the most annoying and arrogant person ever?'

'As a matter of fact—'

A tall blonde, dressed to the nines in a slinky red number, appeared from nowhere and motioned to the bathroom door. Finn stifled his irritation at her giving him the once-over and zeroed in on Serena as she clammed up, took a step back, and dipped her head until that glorious fall of hair veiled her face.

Unsure why it could be, but loathing the way she threw out distress signals, he curled his fingers around her upper arm and tugged her further along the hall to where the dim light imparted privacy.

Except every muscle in her arm tensed beneath his fingers and her gaze bounced off every surface until even *he* half expected someone to pounce.

'Hey, are you okay?'

'Peachy.'

She wrenched free and wrapped both arms across her chest. It was like watching someone erect guard rails.

Okay, so she didn't want to be alone with him. Yet she'd

been fine last night in his bedroom. What had she asked him for? Lights.

'You don't like the dark?' For some reason it made him think back to that odd ramble of Tom's—*'Protect her for me...she's been through enough...'*—and his fists tightened into hard balls of menace.

She bristled with an adorable blend of embarrassment and pique.

'Hey, so you don't like the dark? So what? Neither do I. When I was a kid I used to crawl into bed with my mum during power cuts, for Pete's sake. Some hard-ass Spider-Man I was.'

She blinked over and over, until the fine lines creasing her brow smoothed. 'Spider-Man, huh? Did you have the blue and red outfit too?'

'Sure I did. And the cool web-maker.'

Her small smile lit the corners of the hall. Finn wanted it stronger, brighter.

'Did you have a tutu or a Snow White dress? My baby sister had all that crap.'

She snorted. 'I doubt Snow White wielded a wrench, and I don't expect engine oil would wash out of a tutu very well.'

His every thought slammed to a halt.

Reared by men in a man's world. No mother—he knew from Michael Scott that Serena's mum had died giving birth to her. No sisters.

'Have there been *any* women in your life?'

She gave a blithe shrug but he didn't miss the scowl that pinched her mouth. 'Only my dad's playthings.'

'Ah. I get it.' The narcissistic variety. Or maybe weak, fawning versions Serena would have recoiled from. So naturally she'd kept with the boys, until, 'You feel uncomfortable around women.'

'No!' She kicked her chin up defensively.

Finn cocked one brow and a long sigh poured from her lips.

'I don't know what to say to them, that's all, okay? We have nothing in common.'

'You've never had any girlfriends *at all*?' The notion was so bizarre he couldn't wrap his head around it.

'Not really, no. Tom and I had long-distance schooling, and it was pretty rare to see girls hanging around the circuit.'

Finn kept his expression neutral, conscious that empathy wouldn't sit well with her. Yet all he could think of was his sister, surrounded by girlfriends, and she'd had their mother through her formative years. He dreaded to think what Serena's adolescence had been like. No shopping trips or coming-of-age chats, nor any of that female pampering stuff he'd used to roll his eyes at but which had made Eva fizz with excitement.

He was astonished that Serena had managed without a woman in her life. Had she been allowed to be a girl at all? And why exactly did that make anger contort his guts? They were nothing to one another; only hate coloured her world when she looked at him.

'So you have a sister?' she asked quietly, almost longingly, and his chest cramped with guilt. It didn't seem fair, somehow, that he still had Eva and Serena had no one.

'Yes, I do. Eva.'

Eva—who had suffered greatly from the demise of Libby St George. And what had he done? Turned his back on her, on both of them, and walked away to chase his dreams, his big break. Knowing what they'd go through because he'd seen it all before. He'd left Eva to cope, to watch their beautiful mother slowly fade away.

Finn had let them down. Badly. And, what was worse, he hadn't been the only one. His father, the great Nicky St George, eighties pop-star legend, had left to find solace in many a warm bed. Looking back, Finn still found it hard to believe he'd watched a good man—his childhood hero— break so irrevocably under the weight of heartache. And, while he felt bitterly angry towards his father to this day, he could hardly hate the man when he'd felt the same pain. When he'd let them down too.

Yet still his baby sister loved him. She was all goodness while he was inherently selfish.

Eva. His mind raced around its mental track. Eva would be perfect for Serena. A great introduction to the best kind of women...

Finn stomped on the brakes of his runaway thoughts.

It would be dangerous to take Serena to Eva. Eva might get the wrong idea. Serena might get the wrong idea. *He* might get the wrong idea. He was supposed to be getting rid of her, not fixing her and finding ways to keep her around! What was *wrong* with him?

'Through here.' He beckoned her towards another door. One he pushed wide and held as she warily followed him into one of the small lounges where the private games of the high-flyers were often held.

'Why do I half expect the Monte Carlo Symphony Orchestra to strike up any second?'

'It's the grandeur of the place. It's pretty spectacular.' Oppressive at times, but spectacular nonetheless.

'If you like that kind of thing,' she muttered, with a slick manoeuvre that brought her back flush against another wall.

Musing on why she'd cornered herself again, Finn lounged against the arm of an emerald antique sofa a few feet away and faced her. 'So, what do you fancy for dinner?'

She sniffed, the action wrinkling her little nose. 'I'd rather starve.'

'You've changed your tune pretty quick. Is it a habit of yours? It was only this afternoon you said, "I wouldn't be seen dead" in reference to this very establishment. What changed your mind?'

Pouting those luscious lips, she weighed him up from top to toe, her gaze burning holes in his ten-thousand-pound tux. He felt all but cauterised.

'First off, why don't you tell me why you're avoiding me?'

Because I can't tell you what you want to hear.

'Because every time I look at you I want to make love to that beautiful mouth of yours. It's addictive.' She was like a drug—the prime source of some very intense highs. 'But you don't want that, do you, Seraphina?' he asked, rich and smooth, with a sinful tone he couldn't quell even if he tried.

Up came her stubborn chin. 'No, I don't.'

'Then I would advise you to stay away. Because sooner or later we'll have another repeat of last night.'

It was only a matter of time. Whether she wanted to believe it or not.

From the way her pulse throbbed wildly at the base of her throat and a soft flush feathered her skin he knew she was thinking about their kiss. Was she still tasting him as he could her?

'I don't intend to make the same mistake twice. I know a car crash when I see one,' she said tartly. Then gave herself away by licking her raspberry pout.

She could taste him, all right. He'd also bet she wanted more and loathed herself for it.

Cursing inwardly, he allowed himself the luxury of drinking her in before he made his excuses and left.

Covered in a thin black trench coat, with a high, stiff collar and a straight no-nonsense hem just above the knee, she reminded him of a prissy professor. Though her perfectly sexy knees and her shapely bare calves smothered in luscious ivory skin ruined the imagery. As for her feet…

Finn clenched his jaw and breathed past the grin begging to be let loose.

Oh, man, did he want to see under that coat. More than his next breath.

'Do you like to gamble, Miss Scott? Try your chances with Lady Luck?'

'Not particularly. I'm not so sure I believe in luck.'

Her admission was a prelude to a charge in the air as secrets and lies swirled around them in an electrical storm.

'I'll make a deal with you,' he drawled. *Risky, Finn*—and didn't that just rouse his desire? He chose his next words very, *very* carefully. 'If you do something for me I may grant you one wish. As long as it's in my power to give.'

Up came her chin once more, her grey gaze narrow with scepticism as her need fought hand in hand with obvious discomfort. 'Deal.'

'Show me what you're wearing beneath that coat.'

'Wh…*what*?'

'You heard. Untie that sash, undo those buttons, pull that coat wide and show me.'

Chaotic emotion and energy writhed around inside him.

What he was doing he had no idea. All he knew was that common sense and control took a back seat when he was within five feet of her.

Closing her eyes, she took a deep breath, and the sultry swell of her breasts made heat, fast and furious, speed through his body.

Ah, hell, he should stop her.

Right now.

'A deal is a deal, Miss Scott. You don't strike me as the type to renege.'

She tapped her hands against the ruffle of material at her thigh and slowly, provocatively, tiptoed her fingers up to the knot of her sash.

Finn gritted his teeth as the ribbon-like belt sank to each side of her hips.

Every pop of every button was magnified, the sound echoing off the silk-covered walls, until she gripped the sides of the soft black fabric.

Then she heaved a bashful sigh, rolled her eyes, and pulled the lapels wide, giving him exactly what he was looking for.

'Happy now?' she snapped.

'Ecstatic.' Only Serena would storm into one of the most exclusive casinos in the world wearing a pair of frayed denims cut high on her toned thighs and another quirky

T-shirt—this one ocean blue, with two scuba divers and the words 'Keep Your Friends Close and Your Anemones Closer' riding across her taut stomach.

With no effort whatsoever, she lit up his dark, dark soul.

'What gave me away?' she asked, a hint of petulance smoking her tone.

He pointed his index south. 'Your feet.'

Her gaze followed the direction of his finger. 'What's wrong with my feet?' Her brow furrowed, her head shot back up, eyes slamming into his. 'And what's with that wicked gleam and that grin?'

'I've just never seen you in anything other than biker boots.'

'So?' she snarked. 'One of my dad's ex-lovers gave them to me, I think. This is the first time I've had them on.'

Light crept over marble-grey and Finn hurtled towards lucidity. The reason she wouldn't be seen dead here. The reason she'd shied away from the glamour puss outside the bathroom. Not only did she feel uncomfortable around women, she felt horridly out of place—and yet she'd come here to find him.

Beautiful *and* brave. He'd never wanted her more. And didn't that spell trouble?

'So I'll ask you again,' she groused. 'What's wrong with my feet?'

'Nothing, baby, they're cute.' The last thing he wanted to do was make her feel worse. She didn't have a clue.

'Cute?' she spat. 'Kittens are cute. I am *not* cute. And cut it out with the *baby*. It's driving me nuts!'

'Tell the truth—you love it. Every time I say it you careen into some kind of delightful fluster.'

The nuts part was that she *was* beginning to like it, and she didn't want to like anything he said to her.

'Don't be ridiculous,' she snapped. 'Now it's my turn. I want my wi…'

Her voice trailed off, eyes widening, as he pushed himself

off the sofa-arm and sauntered towards her. While he had every intention of playing fair, it wouldn't hurt to distract her, now, would it? If he tried to kiss her again she would either hit him or bolt. Either exit was fine with him.

When he was up close and personal she raised her head, and Finn caught sight of the wild flutter at the base of her throat.

'I bet you don't even realise you have the most beautiful, elegant décolletage.' He trailed one fingertip down the side of her neck. 'And this skin of yours is a perfectly gorgeous peach colour.' *Yeah, like peaches and cream, to go with that strawberries and cream voice.*

'St…stop saying stuff like that, Finn.'

No.

'Love the T,' he murmured as he brushed down between her breasts with the backs of his fingers, over the creased transfer of frothy waves in a blue ocean—'Keep Your Anemones Closer'. *Sorry, beautiful, not going to happen.*

Down, down he stroked—with fire unfurling at the tops of his thighs—and when he reached her navel—

He growled. Snatched his fingers away and slammed both hands against the wall on either side of her head.

'Wha…what's wrong?'

Finn closed his eyes. 'I need to look.'

'A…at what?'

'You know what. On your stomach.'

A tremble shook her voice. 'Only if you tell me what's wrong with my…my feet.'

Prising his eyes open, he focused on the perpetrators. 'Nothing is wrong. Nothing at all. They're pretty little… ballerina pumps. I think that's what they're called.'

'Do you know you pause when you lie?'

Great.

'Okay, okay. They're slippers.'

Her gorgeous face fell in horror and if she'd been any

other woman he suspected she would have burst into tears. Not Serena.

'They *are*?'

'Cute ones,' he said quickly. 'With little leopard spots on.'

Dismay vaulted into pique and she visibly vibrated before him. 'I refuse to feel stupid just because you know more about women's stuff than I do, considering how many you've had.'

He divined that any figure she could engineer would be highly exaggerated, but still... 'Agreed.' If she felt stupid she wouldn't let him take a peek at her belly button, now, would she?

'Fine. Go on, then. Get it over with. Take a look. But know this: I couldn't care less for your opinion.'

'Liar.' He brushed the pad of his thumb from the corner of his mouth across his bottom lip, eking out the suspense of the moment, then bent his knees and lowered himself into an elegant crouch.

Serena raised the fabric of her T-shirt with an innate feminine sensuality she wasn't even aware she possessed and vicious need clawed at his gut.

One look and he cursed softly.

All the will in the world couldn't have stopped him. Out sneaked his tongue and he licked the small loop and diamond-studded ball.

Cool was the silver against the tip of his tongue, and her soft flesh was a welcome splash of warmth as an aftertaste.

Holy...

She tasted of passion fruit and coconut and something else he couldn't quite catch, so he knew it would torment him.

That was it. He was a goner. He even felt his eyes roll into the back of his head. Wondered if hers were doing the same.

'You got any more?' he asked thickly, nuzzling her navel with the tip of his nose. All the while he was commanding his legs to stand up and back the *hell* away.

'M...more?' she said, or at least she tried to.

The way her midriff quivered he could tell her breathing was as bad as his.

'Piercings.'

'Piercings?'

What was she? A parrot?

'Yes!'

'No. No more…piercings.'

He moaned low in his throat. 'But something else, right?'

Silence. Only the staccato wisp of a desperate moan from her lips.

'Tell me,' he demanded.

So of course she said, 'No.'

'Oh, man, you're killing me, Serena.' Up he came, standing tall to press closer. To crush those gorgeous breasts against his chest.

When was the last time he'd felt like this? Like his old self but astoundingly better because his ever-present guard was low. Risky. *So* risky.

But when was the last time he'd thought about anything but Singapore? In one way it physically hurt to be near her, aware that he caused her pain. But in the next second he was a man again and there was heat. So much heat. Scorching his blood in a rush of need and pure want. Never had he felt anything like it.

Selfish as always, he wanted—no, *needed* one more taste.

'I warned you, baby. You should've left when you had the chance.'

Desperate to savour as much of her as he could, he dived into the heavy fall of her hair and closed the gap until they were nose-tip to nose-tip.

'This is crazy, but—do you *feel* this?' he asked, unable to hide the awe in his voice.

Fighting to keep her eyes open, she shook her head, rubbing his nose with her own. 'No…' she breathed on a hot little pant.

'Good. Me neither.'

Softly, languidly, he brushed his lips over her velvety pink flesh and the pounding of his heart jacked out of rhythm. Then the need that continually clawed at him grew steel-tipped talons and slashed through his gut, demanding he mark her, take her, glut himself on her.

And she was melting. There was no other word for it.

'I'm...' *Hard. So hard.* For the first time in almost a year.

Thought obliterated, he crushed her body into the wall, then slanted his head and deepened his kiss. Like dynamite they ignited, and when she responded with a tentative stroke of her tongue his hands began to shake.

Her mouth was heaven—warm and wet, with the slip and slide of passionate lips—but, greedy as he was, he wanted more. A deeper connection. He longed for her to move, to touch him properly, covet his body with her small hands, be skin-to-skin. *Claim* him. Brand him as her own. Which was not only bizarre but hellishly scary.

Still the need went on. Because he wanted her to feel how hard he was for her, to know what she did to him, how sexy and desirable she was—

Whoosh! The door swung open with a bellow of male voices and they were flung apart as if electrocuted. It was comical in a way. Serena was visibly rattled and he doubted he looked much better. And since when had *that* ever happened?

She whipped the black fabric around her waist, veiling her body, and fumbled with the sash—her jerky movements made his heart thunder in a fiercely savage urge to protect.

'We leave *now*,' he commanded, livid that he'd placed her in this position.

They were halfway to the door when one of the men broke into laughter as he settled at a gaming table.

Serena crashed to a halt. Stared at the man's back. Paled to a ghostly white. And Finn's guts twisted, tying him into knots. 'Hey, baby?' he murmured. 'What's wrong?'

In response she bolted past one of the other guests like a

mare from the starting gate, almost knocking that man off his feet as she virtually ran out the door.

What the...?

By the time he caught up she was galloping down the hallway.

'Serena, stop. *Stop!*'

Edging his way to stand in front of her, before she trampled over half the Casino members, he slipped his finger under her chin and lifted it gently.

'Look at me. Speak to me. Do you know that guy?'

'No.' Hands trembling, she gripped the lapels of his jacket and leaned into him.

Finn could feel her warm breath through his shirt as she burrowed as if starved of affection, and he instinctively pulled her into the tight circle of his arms.

Holding her was like a chorus of pleasure and pain that struck at his guilt but sang a sweet note of solace, and he luxuriated in the feel of her.

'No!' She twisted and rolled her shoulders to wrench free. 'Get off me, Finn. Right now.'

Feet leaden, he took a step back, fists plunging to his sides.

Remorse and mortification darkened the grey hue of her eyes and he swallowed hard, knowing. It was Finn who was the issue here. She was ashamed of wanting him, crestfallen at her reaction to him, horrified she'd kissed him back at all.

Well, then... Considering the destruction he'd caused in his life, it was highly indicative and somewhat poignant that he'd never hated himself more.

CHAPTER SIX

SHE WAS HEARING voices, seeing things. She *must* be. That laugh was dead and buried but still it crawled through her veins like venom.

Gorging on air, she calmed the violent crash of her heart before she completely lost her mind and tried to snuggle into Finn again. *Come on, Serena. Snuggle?* Being weak and needy was not a condition she'd ever aspired to.

Honestly, this night couldn't get any worse. Charging up here to confront him hadn't been the brightest idea, but she'd had an entirely different kind of tongue-lashing in mind.

Forget lethal weapon—the man was a nuclear bomb. And his kiss... *Holy moly.* There she'd been, quite content to pretend their last lip-lock had been an apparition. Why bother to remember when it couldn't possibly have been *that* shockingly good?

Except it *was* that shockingly good. And bad all at the same time.

Her reactions to him were ridiculously extreme. It was as if he flipped a two-way switch inside her—hate or lust. Which just made no sense. She'd kissed men she'd actually liked before and been slammed in a freezer, yet one touch from Lothario here and she burst into flames!

Sheer panic had her scrambling for perspective. Truthfully, she shouldn't feel so disgusted with herself, so humiliated for succumbing to him. Not when the entire female race swooned at those extraordinary cerulean eyes. Expired at that sinful, sensual mouth. And that was before he backed it up with a truckload of charismatic charm.

Serena was just one of many.

Ugh. The idea that she was turning into a woman like one of her dad's playthings made her feel physically sick.

And of course the dirty deed *had* to transpire with her wearing slippers, of all things—just her rotten luck. And Finn knew what they were. Of course he did. He'd probably tugged billions of the things off perfectly feminine feet.

How. Utterly. Mortifying.

At the risk of garnering attention, she whispered furiously, 'Don't you *ever* touch me again. Your hands are not welcome on me.' She was being unfair, she knew she was, but she despised herself for that momentary lapse.

'Noted,' he bit out, his jaw tight enough to crack, and she fancied his broad frame seethed with self-loathing.

Clearly she was losing it.

Serena edged around his broad frame, determined not to notice how he filled out his sinfully suave tuxedo to perfection. 'I have to go. I'll see you in the morning.'

She didn't slow her pace until she was free of the oppressive glitz and glamour, her feet step-step-stepping down the stone slabs of the wide front entrance.

'I'll walk you down to the harbour.'

Finn fell into place beside her, hands stuffed into his trouser pockets, and as if he sensed she was spooked he ground out, 'No arguments.'

It was the second time he'd brandished that arrogant, masculine tone like a swordsman in protective stance and it did something strange to her insides. Made her go all warm and gooey. Which naturally made her every self-defence instinct kick into gear. She wanted to tell him to get lost—preferably on Mars. But something stopped her.

It was that frigid, ominous laughter. Playing in her mind. An endless loop of pain and vulnerability. Vehement enough for her to say, 'Okay…' because in truth she felt infinitely safer with him beside her.

Down the cobbled streets they went, the only sound the *clickety-clack* of his highly polished shoes and the sensual whispers of couples strolling by hand in hand.

As always, the sight made her heart ache. Ache for something she'd never have. Relationship material she was *not*.

Suddenly cold, she wrapped her arms across her chest, and by the time the tang of seawater filled her lungs and the harbour was a glittering stretch before them she was waging an internal war against asking him to stay.

'Thanks for walking with me. I'll be fine from here.'

'Are you sure you'll be okay? Is there anything I can do? Anything you want, Serena?'

Cruel—she was being cruel. The last few months had turned her into a horrible, horrible person but she couldn't curb the truth.

'The only thing I want right now is Tom. He was more than my brother—he was my friend.' And she didn't want to be alone.

But you are alone, Serena, and you always will be. What doesn't kill you makes you stronger.

'I know,' he said, his voice deep and low, tainted with sombre darkness. 'Believe me, I know.'

It was a voice she'd never heard before. One that made her stop. Pause. Wonder at the torment engulfing his beautiful blue eyes.

'I would do anything to turn back the clock. Anything to change the words I said. If only I'd just told him no when he asked to come out with me. Countless times I've wished for just that.'

As if he'd hit her with a curveball, she swayed on her feet.

The way he'd phrased it, so simply, had brought it all down to choices. Tom's choice in asking to follow his hero. Finn's choice in allowing him to.

Strange to think how the twists of fate intertwined with free will.

Every day they lived a voyage of discovery, moved through life based on choices like forks in the road. They peered down all the options, considered, weighed the risks, finally made a choice—some good, some bad. Some affecting no one but themselves. The worst affecting those they loved. But all of them defining. Forging who they were.

She'd made hundreds of choices in her lifetime and had one major regret. A choice that had affected her dad's life, Tom's life too, until the day he'd died. One made when she'd been naïve about her place in the world, no more than a girl, but a disastrous choice even so.

'I would do anything to turn back the clock.'

Serena would too.

Instead she lived with the guilt, struggled with it, controlled it. Recognised it when she saw it in others. This time she saw it in Finn—such depth of emotion—her first glimpse in...forever.

First? No. She'd been struck with shards of his shattering façade since last night.

Glimpse? No. He looked *devastated*. Seething with a darkness she truly believed was pain.

'Finn?' Who *was* this man? Thawing the ice and hate she'd packed in her chest. 'Oh, Finn, you really liked him, didn't you?' He was grieving too.

Punching his fists deep into his trouser pockets, he cast his gaze over the moonlit ripple of the ocean. 'He was a good kid.'

Knowing this was her chance, she begged him, 'Tell me what happened that night. Your version. Please. My dad just keeps saying there was a storm and he fell overboard during the night, but when I checked there were no weather warnings, no reports.'

His brow etched in torment, he closed his eyes momentarily. 'It was…' His throat convulsed. 'Unexpected. There is nothing more to tell.'

His tone was as raw as an open wound and she ached for him, but— 'Why do I think there is?'

'Because you need to let go.' He shoved frustrated hands through his thick blond hair. 'Otherwise you'll find no peace, Serena. I promise you.'

A cool rush of sea air washed over her in a great wave and she crossed her arms over her chest, then curled her fingers around her upper arms and rubbed at the sudden prickle of gooseflesh.

'Peace? I don't know what that feels like. I never have.'

Finn stilled, watching her, predator-like. Then anger crept across his face, dark and deadly, and her pulse surged erratically at her wrist.

'Have you been hurt? In the past?' he asked, almost savagely.

It was as if his genetic make-up had been irrevocably altered and she could feel the ferocious fury of an animal growling through him. Not to harm—no, no. To protect.

She shouldn't like that. She really shouldn't.

'Serena?'

'I… Well…' She bit her top lip to stem the spill of her secrets.

Ridiculous idea. It had to be the way he visibly swelled beneath his suave attire as if to shield her. It made her heart soften and she couldn't afford that. Just the thought rebooted her self-preservation instincts and she dodged.

'To be honest, Finn, I'm not one for dwelling on the past.' She didn't want to remember being naïve and weak and broken. Didn't want Finn to suspect she was any of those things. She refused to be vulnerable to him. To any man ever again.

More importantly, she was over it. She'd made a life for herself. A good life. True, being initiated into the dark realms the world had to offer at fourteen years old was not conducive to relationships and all the messy complexities that came with them.

It was hard to trust, to let go. And, while she'd vowed her past wouldn't define her, or cripple her life with fear, any attempts she'd made at intimacy had been a dishearteningly dismal experience. She'd chosen a wonderfully sweet safe guy but she'd felt distanced somehow. Detached. Compounded by her blatant lack of femininity, no doubt. But she had her work, which she loved, and her team kept her from touching the very depths of loneliness. And if the tormented shadows still haunted her once in a while she fought them with all her might.

Feeling that infusion of bravado, she lifted her chin. 'Anyway, do I look like the kind of woman someone could easily mess with?' She hoped not. She'd spent years building her defences after all.

Finn slowly shook his head and his fierce scowl was tempered into a decadent curve of his lips as he murmured what sounded like, 'That's my girl.'

Their eyes caught...held...and Serena would have sworn she actually felt the odd dynamic of their relationship take a profound twist.

Before she knew it more words flooded over her tongue— a chaotic, unravelling rush she couldn't seem to stop.

'When I look at you I want to blame you, hate you.' And hadn't it been easier to blame Finn instead of just accepting it as a tragic accident from which no justice could be reaped? 'But on the back of those thoughts comes the guilt, the self-censure, because he asked *me* to go out with him that night and I wouldn't.'

She'd been horribly selfish, hating the social scene, knowing she didn't fit in, so she'd told him to go, to have fun.

'If I'd gone out with him he wouldn't have asked *you*.' Misery poured from her heart. 'I was such a coward.' Oh, God, could it have been her fault?

Finn surged forward, raised his arm and brushed a lock of hair from her brow so tenderly her heart throbbed.

'You can't take responsibility for someone else's actions, baby. He was old enough to make his own decisions.'

'Well, then I should've persuaded him to take professional swimming lessons—' Her voice cracked. 'Something. Anything.'

'Again, you can't make people do what they don't want to. You think he'd honestly want you to blame yourself like this?'

'No,' she whispered. Tom would go crazy if he saw her right now.

Crazy? She gave a little huff. If Tom knew she was being cruel to Finn he would go berserk. Finn had been his hero. He'd talked about him constantly. And hadn't *that* driven her insane too? Ensuring he was never far from her mind. Taunting her. Creating more anger. Powering more hate. But that wasn't Finn's fault. It was hers. Because she'd never understood her unruly all-consuming reactions to such a wild player. He was anything *but* safe.

'How did it happen?' she asked, suddenly weary. 'Were you there? All I want to know is that he didn't suffer.'

A muscle ticked in his jaw and he took a large step back, filching her heat. 'I was...asleep. It was the middle of the night.'

A black blend of torment and bone-wrenching guilt stole the colour from his beautiful face and from nowhere she wanted to throw her arms around him. He was hurting so badly. Like a wounded animal. It was like being tossed back in time, staring at her own reflection. She couldn't bear it.

Trembling, she reached for his hand, the despair and loneliness she'd suffered in the last months calling to her—reaching out for his, to share it. To comfort and be comforted. A craving she'd stifled for months.

All the torment. The guilt suffocating her. Suffocating him. When she'd thought he didn't care she'd wanted to punish him endlessly. Yet he'd buried it just as she had. And where was it getting them? Fate had dealt them a cruel card and unless they moved on all she could see lining the road ahead was endless misery.

Let it go...

Her fingers met his skin and as if she'd zapped him with three thousand volts he jolted backwards.

'I've already warned you once tonight, Serena,' he said roughly. 'You touch me right now and I'll lose it. Won't be able to stop myself from wanting more.'

The memory of him crouched before her, his hot gaze locked on her lower abdomen, his warm breath teasing over her flesh, sprang up in her mind's eye and heat drenched her body like a deluge of tropical rain.

'I...I don't understand you. Are you still trying to distract me or something? Because you're wasting your time, Finn, I'm not going anywhere.'

He rubbed at his temple as if she was giving him a migraine. 'I'm beginning to realise that.'

'Good. But I still can't fathom why you want more from me. I'm not—'

His turbulent gaze crashed into her. 'Not beautiful? Yes, you are. Sexy? More than anyone I've ever met.'

Yeah, right. 'I meant I'm not a woman. Not feminine—stuff like that.'

'Of course you are—'

'Er...hello? Slippers?' While *he* looked wicked and gorgeous in his devilish tux.

'In your own unique way.'

'No. I'm not.' *Was she?* 'Nor do I want to be.' Unveiling that secret part of her would only bring more vulnerabilities. Weakness.

Finn shook his head, his mouth shaping for speech. Then he seemed to think better of it. 'Listen; while the best place for you is far away from me, we have to work together, *boss-lady*. At least until the end of the season.'

Was he saying he wasn't staying with the team? He must know her dad would want him to.

'I know that.' The strike of her conscience made her wince. 'About the boss thing...'

The ghost of a smile softened his sinful mouth. 'A slight exaggeration on your part, Miss Scott?'

'Could've been,' she posed lightly.

'You've got balls, Serena, I'll give you that.'

Their eyes locked once more and she held her breath. Wishing she could read him better. Hating her lack of experience. By the time he tore his eyes free she felt dizzy from the lack of oxygen.

'Regardless, we'll still be seeing a lot of each other, so I suggest we endeavour not to end up alone. Unless...'

'Unless?'

He shifted on his glossy feet. 'Unless you ever need...a friend.' He scrubbed his nape with the palm of his hand. A bit uneasy. A whole lot handsome. 'That's what you said, wasn't it? That you'd lost a friend too? So if you ever need one I'll be there.'

Oh, great. Now he was being all thoughtful. A little bit wonderful. The *last* thing she needed.

Friendship was a terrible idea. They clashed like titans. But she wasn't about to throw his offer in his face. She didn't have the heart. 'Okay. It's a deal.'

With a brief nod he turned to walk away.

'Finn?'

'Yeah?'

Am I truly beautiful to you? Did you mean it?

'Don't forget,' she said. 'You owe me a wish.'

Finn stripped his jacket from his body, yanked the black tie from his collar and slung them across the caliginous suite. Then he flopped atop the bed, face down, his insides raw and aching from being clawed to shreds.

Withholding the truth hammered at his conscience, making his temples pound until his vision blurred and he prayed for peaceful slumber. Not that he deserved it. The past was catching up with him, slowly but surely.

He'd been so close to telling her everything. Battling with a promise made, an investigation that could blow wide any day, and an insight that she'd been through her own version of hell.

What had happened to his brave little tigress? She'd cleverly derailed him and he'd never met anyone who'd managed that feat. Were they talking emotional or physical hurt, here? Though in reality maybe it was best he didn't know.

The imagery taunting his mind made him want to snarl and lash out—vicious, savage with the need for revenge. It made his guts ache with a peculiar primal need to take her in his arms and hold her to him, protect her. Kiss her tenderly, passionately, over and over—make her feel like a real woman.

How was he going to keep his hands off her if she took his offer of friendship?

Exhaustion pulsed through his bones and darkness called to him like an old friend, dragging him into the depths where only nightmares pulsed to life...

Singapore, September, eight months earlier

'Wakey-wakey, pretty boy.'

Derision leaked from the hoarse oriental twang as the sound of heavy boots clomping over concrete, cracking the grit and filth beneath inch-thick soles, penetrated the lethargic smaze in which his mind wandered.

Hair like the heart of a ruby...fire in its most dangerous form...

The twang grew louder. 'How are we feeling today?' But it was the jangle of a loaded key ring slapping against a military toned thigh that finally roused his head from its cushioned spot on the exposed brick wall.

His backside numb from sitting on the damp floor for hours on end, he conspicuously flexed the legs outstretched in front of him, knowing what was to come.

After all, he could set his watch by these guys—if he still had it. As it was, the rare platinum timepiece now graced one of the guard's thick, brawny wrists.

Four and a half million he'd been paid to wear that watch—to have his face plastered on every billboard from here to Timbuktu.

Easy money.

Exactly what these men wanted from him. He could have coped with that if it wasn't for the kid in the next cell. If that kid hadn't been in the wrong place at the wrong time and got dragged into this godforsaken mess.

He smacked his head off the pitted brick, wondering once again if they'd get out of here alive. Wherever 'here' was. Some place near the ocean, if the sporadic bites of salt water were anything to go by.

He craved a glance at the skyline. Light. Space. Or, better yet, an endless track to drive down, to escape from reality. As it was, he had too many hours to think—an overrated and highly dangerous pastime. If he wasn't imagining the peaceful waters of stunning grey eyes regrets suffocated him as they shadowed his mind like tormented souls.

The mistakes he'd made in his life. The hearts he'd broken in his youth. The way he'd abandoned his mother and Eva. What if he never had the chance to say sorry?

Chest so tight he could scarcely breathe, he stuffed the lot to the back of his mind, where all the other emotional garbage was, and let it fester. Concentrated on what he was capable of dealing with—Mr Happy in the khaki combats, who seemed to be snarling at him.

'There is something wrong with your tongue?'

Yeah, as a matter of fact there was. It hadn't tasted water for two days. But he'd guess Brutus, here, just wanted his answer.

How was he feeling? As if he'd had his insides scooped out and then shoved back in. With a blunt spoon.

'Great. Never felt better. Your hospitality is second to none.'

The you'll-pay-for-that smirk should have made him regret his smart mouth, but he had to keep their focus on *him*. *Always* on him.

'I am pleased to hear it.' The guard paused outside the kid's cell and Finn felt the familiar toxic churn of foreboding right in the pit of his empty stomach. 'And your friend?'

Already halfway up from his cosy spot on the floor, Finn almost lost his precarious stance. 'He's sick. Can't even walk. So leave him alone.' Then he smoothed the edge off his harsh tone and kicked up his lips, offering the legendary St George smile as he straightened to his full height. 'It's me you want, anyway. Isn't that right?'

Another smirk. Another churn of unease and sickening revolt in his stomach.

'Boring when they don't fight back.'

'There you go, then. Let me out of here.' He jerked his chin towards the kid. 'The view is depressing.' Or it would be for the kid pretty soon.

'Finn?' Tom croaked. 'Let me—'

'Shut up, kid.' Every muscle in his body protested as he coerced his legs forward as if two of his ribs *weren't* cracked and his shoulder *wasn't* dislocated. Piece of cake. 'I'm feeling cooped up in here.' His door swung wide. 'Give him some water, would you?'

The guard grinned, flashing a less than stellar set of teeth, eyes brimming with calculation. As if he knew something Finn didn't. As if the last four days had been foreplay to the main event.

Darkness seeped through the cracks in his mind and threatened to rise like some ugly menacing storm. 'You leave the kid alone—you hear me? Or no money.'

The laugh that spilled from those blood-red lips made his guts wrench tighter.

'Boss says the only thing I leave alone is your pretty face,' the guard said, and slapped said face with enough force to sting. 'Get moving.'

'Speaking of my generous host, I want to talk to him again.'

'Your wish is my command.'

Somehow he doubted that. Nevertheless, ten minutes later a big palm pushed on his shoulder—the dislocated one, thank you very much—and he fought the wince as he was slammed down into a black plastic chair in the corner of a room that looked like an interrogation hotspot out of a gritty cop show. But, nope, this was no TV set. Proof of which sat in the chair opposite, with a rickety steel-framed table separating them.

Face-to-face with his captor, it wasn't in Finn's nature to beat around the proverbial bush, so he kicked off today's festivities.

'Let's barter,' he managed to say through a throat that felt serrated with sticks. 'I'll trade you another five million if you let him go. *Now.*'

Eyes as black as his soul and sunk into a battered, rock-hewn face stared back at him. 'That's quite an offer, Mr St George. But I was thinking of a different kind of bartering altogether.'

'I'm getting tired of these games. What exactly is it you want?'

'Right now I want you to make a choice, racer-boy. The first of many.'

Behind him, the iron door ground open with a chilling squeal and a frigid bite swept through the room—so cold his bones turned to ice. The kid was behind him. He knew it.

'Forget choices. Make it another ten mill and let. Him. Go.'

'You don't like him being touched, do you, pretty boy?' he said silkily—in striking contrast to the sharp crack of knuckles that caromed around the room. 'So shall I play with him? Or will you?'

Finn's breath sawed in and out of his lungs. 'Twenty. That will be sixty million, transferred from my Swiss bank account within the hour. You can do what the hell you like with me. Deal?'

CHAPTER SEVEN

MONTREAL BASKED IN the warmth of a glorious dusk, the sky a canvas of fluffy spiralling ribbons tinged with orange and red, with only a blaze of yellow on the curve of the earth, where the sun kissed the horizon.

Its beauty failed miserably to improve her ugly mood.

'You'd better be in, Finn,' Serena muttered as she stormed across the endless blanket of tarmac towards his glossy black motor home.

Never mind the prescient darkness that had clung to her skin for two weeks since Monaco, like some kind of impending doom, Michael Scott—aka *dear old Dad*—had just pulled a number on her! As if the day hadn't been enough of a stress-fest.

The day? Who was she kidding? The last two weeks, working with Mr Death-Defyer, had been a roller coaster named persecution; emotions had dipped and dived all over the place, to stretch her patience endlessly. Was it any wonder she could hear the clang of looming disaster?

Still, she'd never forget this afternoon as long as she lived.

Another close shave as Finn scraped second place after going silent on the pit-lane channel for over two minutes. Heart in her throat, she'd snatched the headset from the chief engineer in the end. Not exactly the done thing, but she'd had to snap him out of it somehow.

He was getting worse. Darker. Harder. Taking unnecessary risks no other man would dare to chance. Why? She couldn't understand it. Unless… Unless Serena had made him worse. By storming into his life and throwing Tom's death in his face when he'd been trying to deal with the loss in his own way. Burying it. Just as she had.

It boggled the mind to think they had something in common.

God, she felt sick.

But had *he* been worried when he'd nearly obliterated himself? Heavens, no. While she'd popped migraine pills like chocolate drops he'd supplicated and beguiled the masses with his glib tongue and legendary rakish smile, standing atop the podium as if life was a fun park and darker emotions were aberrant to him. When she knew they were anything but!

Then—*then* he'd swaggered into the Scott Lansing garage, again, and drawled in that sinfully rich, amused voice, 'What do you think, baby? Was I awesome?'

As if he *hadn't* just phased out while driving at over two hundred miles per hour!

Fist balled, she stomped up the metal steps and rapped on his door until her knuckles stung.

If she was an ace at burying pain and masking it with a brave face he was a pro—a grand virtuoso. But now Serena could see it. Feel his darkness more acutely.

Oftentimes behind the charming, irrepressible smile lurked a guilt-drenched agony she still couldn't bear.

Last night hadn't helped matters either. Bored—okay, plain nosey—she'd searched the internet for a peek of his sister and got a lot more than she'd bargained for. Not only was Eva Vitale the most beautiful woman she'd ever seen, but together with Finn she ran a huge charity for breast cancer in honour of their mother. Another death that must have crippled him.

By the time she'd trawled through all the articles and spotted the Silverstone driving day he held every year for sick

and disabled children she'd cringed at all the heartless, dis-
honourable comments she'd perpetually tossed in his face.

The thought that she'd been so prejudiced against his
type, his Casanova proclivities—enough to use him as an
easy scapegoat for Tom's death—was making her seriously
dislike herself.

The door opened on a soft swish to reveal the man himself, wearing a deep red polo shirt—*yum*—and a pair of
washed-out stomach-curling jeans riding low on his lean
hips.

As her gaze touched his bare toes that delicious drawl
rumbled over her. 'Do I meet with your approval this evening, Miss Scott?'

Her heart thundered like a freight train through her chest
and she crossed her arms over her breasts before it burst
through her skin. 'You'll do.'

The ghost of a smile softened his sinful mouth—only to
veer into a scowl as he searched her face. 'What's wrong?
Has something happened?'

Yeah, I feel wretched.

This was a stupid, stupid idea, she thought for the millionth time. Fair enough doing practice laps and talking
designs, but to come to his trailer? She was making their
awkward truce personal and she knew it.

'Can I come in?'

His eyes said, *Do you have to?* His mouth said, 'Sure.'

Unconvinced, she battled with the urge to turn around
and flee. But he'd offered, hadn't he? To be a friend if she
needed one? And maybe, just maybe, he needed one too.

She was worried about him. Her conscience pleaded with
her to help him before he well and truly did some harm.
She just didn't know how. While she knew tons of men, she
hadn't felt ready to spontaneously combust with any of them
as she did with Finn. *So just ignore it, like you have for the
last four years!*

Sucking in a courageous breath, Serena followed him into

the spanking new motor home—all sharp lines of glass and steel alongside huge cushy leather sofas.

'Nice place. Biggest and best on the lot. If I hadn't heard the endless man-muck around the pits—' she was *not* about to admit he was dubbed the world's greatest lover '—I would think your penchant for size compensated for some kind of deficiency.'

He flashed his sexy suggestive smile and her knees turned to hot rubber. 'Nothing lacking in that department, I promise you.'

'I'll take your word for it,' she muttered. Meaning it. Only to curse blue when her traitorous mind provided her with an image of the first time she'd ever seen him in the flesh, bar-boxer-shorts-naked, strolling into his bathroom. Where Serena had been… *Oh, God.*

A tingling flush crept up her neck until she felt impossibly hot. And the idea that she looked like some gauche ninny made her vibrate with pique.

'Uh-oh. I sense trouble.' Finn leaned against the slash of the kitchen bench, gripped the ledge on either side of his hips and crossed one ankle over the other. 'Okay, baby, spill it.'

Baby. *Baby.* She had to stop dissolving in a long, slow melt when he called her that!

'I'm…' Shifting on her feet, she eyed the door. South America was wonderful at this time of year. Maybe—

'Enraged? Incensed? Hopping mad? Splenetic? Thoroughly bent out of shape?'

'You swallowed a thesaurus, or something?'

'Nah, it's that school I went to. You know—the one that specialises in breeding the most arrogant and annoying people ever?' he said, flinging her words back at her.

'As you can see, I'm rolling around the floor laughing.'

He grinned.

She sighed. Glanced at the door again. Wondered why she felt hideously exposed. Sharing woes and asking for help wasn't weak or too feminine, was it? She didn't enjoy giving men the impression she was weak—it was like hand-delivering an invitation to be messed with.

Oh, to hell with it. 'My dad just decided not to launch the prototype at Silverstone.'

'Why not?'

A tinge of anger fired in his eyes. One that made her feel infinitely better. Even though her bad funk was technically *his* fault.

Because Finn here had officially earned the title 'too wild and problematic' to handle her multimillion-pound proto-type. And she was angry. Noooo. She was upset. There—she'd admitted it, and miraculously the sky hadn't caved in.

'Doesn't matter the reason. His decision is final.'

Next year wasn't so far away. *It felt like forever.* It wasn't as if it would never happen. There was really no need for her to be so…devastated. 'Point is, he has a brunette over there, and I refuse to play nice when I feel—'

'Like someone peed in your biker boots?'

'Exactly.'

One side of his mouth kicked up ruefully before his focus drifted to the window, far into the distance, as if he'd virtu-ally left the room.

Angst crawled through her stomach and Serena gnawed her top lip.

Yes, she was crushed, but she could easily have gone to a hotel. It was a convenient excuse and she knew it. Some-how she had to slide him back on track.

Letting go of a long, soft sigh, she sprinkled some can-dour on her remorse.

If she'd been courageous enough to look into her heart, to face her own fears, she would have accepted that culpa-bility lay with fate. Otherwise she couldn't possibly have kissed Finn with everything she was. And, if she wanted to be brutally, painfully honest, blaming him had been a grand excuse to hate him even more. Since the moment she'd laid eyes on him he'd stirred a hornets' nest of inadequacies to sting her pride and spawn desires that defied logic. Reason.

Inadequacies she'd been slammed up against from when she was nine years old—ribbed for being 'too girly' to play—and had stolen a pair of blunt scissors to hack off her hair.

Desires she'd always had to force, coerce, to do her bidding. Determined her past would not define her.

Disaster.

Until Finn. Who had never failed to spark every female cell in her body to ignite. The sexual pull of his velvet gaze roving over her when he thought she wasn't looking jacked her pulse. Made her dream about the firm, sinful stroke of his hands moving over her skin and the hot drive of his tongue between her lips. Then came the heat, spearing through her veins like arrows of fire.

She didn't want her heart to thump when he was near or for weakness to spread through her limbs. He was still a Casanova. A prolific player.

He took a long, sensual pull of water from a tall glass bottle and she watched his smooth jaw work, his sexy throat convulse, and knew this was a stupid, stupid idea. *Tough.*

'So, can I stay here?'

'No!' he choked. A distressed noise followed by a splutter. A cough. A hard swallow and watering eyes. 'I don't do sleepovers.'

Her mouth going slack, she wasn't sure which to process first. The fact that he didn't do sleepovers with his women or the fact he thought she wanted to 'sleep' with him!

'I didn't ask you if you did. I asked you if I could hang out here while you go out and do your Lothario thing.' Okay, she was digging for info, but right now she didn't care. 'You know—borrow your place. Like friends do.'

Wincing inwardly, she hung on his reaction as she played the friend card, unsure if the tight knot in her stomach wanted him to pick it up or discard it.

'I was planning on staying in most of the night.'

'Oh.'

Come to think of it, of late there'd been no kiss-and-tell stories. No rumours of orgies or nightclub antics. Half of her gloried in the idea that he was abstaining from his play-boy shenanigans and the other half hated the suspicion that he was becoming reclusive, withdrawing from the world even more.

For pity's sake, the man had her tearing herself apart!

Finn scrubbed a palm over the back of his neck. 'Fine. You can hang out here. For a little while.'

'I've never seen a "fine" such as yours right now, Finn.' At his quizzical expression, she elaborated. 'Like I'm stick-ing hot needles down your fingernails.'

His knuckles bleached white as they gripped the lip of the bench. 'Probably because that's what it feels like trying to keep my hands off you.'

A loaded pause sparked in the air. 'Seriously?'

'Oh, you're happy now?'

Maybe. It wasn't so bad resisting him if he felt the same. Maybe he hadn't been lying to her. Maybe he did find her beautiful after all.

Her heart smiled. 'I'll be even happier if you feed me and let me beat you on your games console.' *Friend stuff.*

He snorted. 'In your dreams, baby.'

She had the feeling that was exactly where he'd be tonight. In her dreams. Centre stage. Just as he had been last night. And every other night she could remember.

'You have until ten o'clock to triumph and prove your console supremacy, then I'm going out.'

'Oh.' That was *not* disappointment in her voice. Certainly not.

Finn cocked an arrogant brow and tilted his head, as if she'd presented him with a puzzle he couldn't quite figure out. 'I'll make you a deal.'

'I'm not keen on your deals. Last time I ended up—' *Ohh,* there it went. Stomach flipping over…

'Getting your belly button piercing licked?'

Hello, heatwave—blasting her from all angles as the incredible sensation of his hot mouth on her skin flicked over her on replay.

'It wasn't the most disgusting experience in the world.'

So you can do it again if you like. No—no, he could *not*. It was a terrible idea. Crazy to think she was hurtling towards a lack of self-preservation as diabolical as his.

That legendary beautiful smile touched his lips and he raised one hand to scratch at his jawline. 'Deal is—if you beat me I'll take you with me.'

His grin said he was perfectly safe. That she didn't have a hope in hell of winning. Obviously he didn't want her going with him at all. Which naturally flipped every one of her excitable curiosity switches.

Poor guy. She almost felt sorry for him.

He'd been thrashed. By a girl.

Totally and utterly thrashed at supercars, tennis, football and loaded weapons—repeatedly. Then he'd fed her and fetched her soft drinks. Before she'd zonked out on the sofa in an alluring puddle of colour and vulnerability—the latter hitting him smack-bang in the solar plexus.

Seraphina Scott was extraordinary in every single way, and if he didn't give her a good shake pronto he was liable to kiss her awake like Sleeping Beauty. If he was any kind of prince material he would. As it was he'd lied to her repeatedly and lusted after her repeatedly.

Unfortunately some idiot had suggested he was friend material, and though it scared the crap out of him—because he wasn't the most reliable bloke on the planet, and his own sister could vouch for that—he fully intended to stick by his word. It was the least he could do after he'd caused her so much pain, despite the fact it was the equivalent of flinging himself onto the track lane mid-race.

The fact was, she fed his wildness. Unearthed all kinds of

feral, animalistic instincts until need was a constant claw that slashed his insides. Not just craving the heat of her sweet, supple body, but wanting to protect her at all cost, to touch that desolate tinge in her grey gaze.

She was a lonely soul right now.

It took one to know one. He'd been surrounded by people all his life, and yet soaked in a bone-deep loneliness he found impossible to shake.

Yeah, and impossible to understand too.

Easily bored, he relished variety. *Every day with Serena would be as unique as she was*, a little voice whispered. He told that little voice to shut up. It was being controlled by his libido and for once he wasn't listening.

Finn stared at her for a long moment, curling a strand of her hair around his finger. How could anyone even resist her? How long was it going to take before he snapped and crossed the bridge from friends to lovers? *An eternity*, his conscience told him, *because it's never going to happen. You're supposed to be keeping her safe, remember?*

'Hey, Sleeping Beauty.' He flipped his hand over to check his watch. 'It's nine-thirty and we have a date.'

With her sinuous stretch and a sultry writhe her T-shirt inched upwards until that sexy-as-hell diamond piercing winked at him.

Just like that an airlock cinched his chest. 'Come on, spitfire, get a shake on.' *Before I take that silver loop between my lips, flick it with my tongue and suck it into my mouth. Then I'll tear those jeans off and lick all the way down to your clit. Damn.*

'Or maybe I'll just go by myself.' *Way better idea.*

'I'm coming, I'm coming,' she murmured, in that gorgeous, husky sleep-drenched voice.

He growled long and low. This was such a bad idea. What had possessed him to gamble with her? No one had ever beaten him. Ever. He should've known this minx would throw him for a loop—which only made him want her even more! *So cancel. Tell her something. Anything.*

The problem was he was already living one lie, and the thought of customising another pierced his guts as if they were twisted in barbed wire. Add in the suspicion that today's racing blip—courtesy of a flashback like no other— had totalled her aspirations of launching her prototype at Silverstone and he could never tolerate it.

'Where are we going?' She swung her legs off the leather couch, sat upright and shook out her hair until those spectacular ruby-red flames blazed down her back.

'Here,' he croaked, grabbing two caps from the marble bench and tossing one in her lap. 'Put this on.'

'Incognito?' Her grey eyes bolted to his, sparkled with excitement.

It was an effervescence that wasn't going to last long. Or was it? Continually she threw him, and this little jaunt might be just what she needed.

In a sudden burst of self-honesty he acknowledged that the temptation to take her had arrived shortly after the tickets. But the subject matter had made him pause. She was prudish at times, yet inquisitive at others—the delightful memory of her ear crushed against the bedroom door on his yacht came to mind—and he'd flirted with the idea that her past experiences were slim and less than stellar.

Meanwhile here he was, a veritable connoisseur in the erotic arts of passion and seduction, impervious to being knocked off his feet, suddenly disturbed—no, downright daunted—because this woman could easily take his legs from under him.

It took him five minutes to lock up, usher Serena round to the storage compound and heft the double doors wide.

Click went the automatic lights, flooding the space with fluorescence, blinding him momentarily as he waited for...

Her swift inhalation. A deep, rapturous moan. One that nearly brought him to his knees.

Did she *have* to be the hottest woman on the planet?

'*Ohhh*, yeah,' she breathed, her sultry voice loaded with salacious hunger for his latest toy. 'Your taste is impeccable, Finn. All that horsepower makes me twitchy. I think I'm about to have the ride of my life.'

Finn closed his eyes. He was doomed.

CHAPTER EIGHT

SERENA WAS DOOMED.

Finn had driven her across the city behind the wheel of his high-spec, custom-made, invitation-only sports car, slamming her to the edge of the hot zone. Her hormones were frantic as she imagined him making love with the same intensity—with an inordinate skill and a passionate appreciation for the machine in his hands.

The way he smoothed the leather of the steering wheel with an amorous touch, curled his long fingers around the gearstick with a firm, sensual grip... She'd shuddered with pleasure just watching him.

Now, seated in a super-comfy armchair in a magnificent tent in the middle of Montreal, she was right back on edge. A thrumming mass of expectation.

From the outside the structure appeared like a giant theatrical dome, with multiple conical peaks that soared into the sky in a colourful array of blue and yellow stripes—reminiscent of Arabian nights. And inside the capacious space rivalled the outside's awe factor with a distinct flare of class and luxury. It was the type Serena liked—more avant-garde than ostentatious, cast by the heights of technology for performers to achieve mind-boggling feats. It was exciting and thrill seeking. Definitely her thing.

Something awesome was about to happen, and anticipation fired through her veins like gasoline sparking to ignite.

The dark-haired man sitting on the other side of Finn suddenly turned to face him. 'You're real familiar. Have we met before?'

Serena stifled a smile. She'd expected to lounge in some VIP suite, and being one of the masses was more scintillating than ever. Adding a kick of danger that they'd be discovered.

With the black caps pulled low on their foreheads and dressed in T-shirts and jeans—Finn in a yummy buttery black leather jacket, collar flipped high, and Serena in a dark blue hoodie—they created a perfect image of friends out for kicks.

Finn smiled, all charismatic charm, and held out his hand for an old-boy shake. 'I'm sure I would have remembered you if I had, sir. It's a pleasure.'

It struck her then. In many ways he was a showman himself. Although he blended seamless confidence and ease in any situation, she fancied he adapted to his surroundings, even altered his accent to fit. A veritable chameleon.

It was a talent she could only marvel at with no small amount of envy. Yet she couldn't quite figure out why he felt the need. Why not just be himself?

She could only presume, from the way he blocked his emotions, it was some kind of survival technique—and, let's face it, they'd both been reared on fame and fortune so she knew all about those. Except where she'd shunned it he'd danced beneath the limelight, albeit somewhat distanced by not being his true self. It was as if he preferred to be untouched by everyone around him. Now, *that* was something she definitely understood. Opening up wasn't easy. It invited all sorts of pain, disappointment and heartache.

But, more profoundly, what seriously blew her mind was the stranger who came into view when Finn ditched his façades. *That* man was the most fascinating of all.

It was the man who'd made her spaghetti in his kitchen—the one who'd tucked her unruly hair behind her ear, pouted when he'd lost at the video games, the one who seemed perfectly happy to hang out with 'normal' folk and swig cola.

As for the secretive girly smile on her face—that was down to the way he seemed more content. Not so restless and edgy. No dark pain in his eyes tonight. So any regret she'd harboured about going to him earlier in the evening had flown by the wayside.

'Hey!' the man next to him said. 'I know where I've seen you before. On the TV. You're that guy.'

Serena bit down on her lips and held her breath, curious to see if he'd protect his privacy, give them this one night. Craving the real him for a bit longer.

Finn raised his chin, his bewildered expression worthy of an Oscar-winning actor. 'Who?'

'The one who races them fast cars.'

Frowning, Finn turned to face her, his voice thick and deep enough to carry a perfect American drawl. 'Hey, baby, do I look like that race-car driver?'

Suddenly slap-happy, as if she'd had one too many beers, Serena glanced past Finn to the stranger. 'That British guy?' she asked incredulously.

With a dubious flush, the other man shrugged. 'He could be.'

'No way.' Shaking her head, she leaned back against the pad of her chair. 'He's weird-looking. And his eyes…' She deliberately pulled a shudder up her spine.

Finn cocked one dark blond brow, excused himself graciously, then twisted his mighty fine torso and leaned into her.

'What's wrong with his eyes?'

'They're weird. Cerulean blue and yet sometimes…' She left him dangling for a few blissful seconds in an effort to get him back for all the times he'd toyed with her.

'Sometimes…?' he demanded.

'They change colour. Gleam in a feral kind of way. Hypnotic.'

'Hypnotic?' he murmured silkily, his skin flushed beneath the shadowy peak of his cap. 'Maybe it depends what he's looking at.'

Their gazes caught, held in timeless suspension, and the pull tugged at the base of her abdomen until warmth flooded her knickers.

A groan ripped from his throat as if he knew. Could smell the scent of her arousal.

'And...' She smothered her lips with moisture. 'He has this serious animalistic vibe going on. He *growls*.'

Sculpted in black leather, his broad shoulders rose and fell as the tempo of his breathing escalated. 'Do you like it?'

'I love it.' She'd been lured, ensnared, and now she wanted to be caught—

No. *No!* God, what was going on with her? She had to cut this out. Think *friends*.

The hand that lay on his muscular thigh fisted and he pulled back an inch or three. 'Do you know what Seraphina means, Miss Scott?'

She gave a little shake of her head and he elaborated.

'The fiery one.'

Right now that made perfect sense.

'So be careful that you don't get set ablaze. You don't want to get burned, do you, Seraphina?'

'You *burn* women?' she whispered, sounding more intrigued than appalled—and how ridiculous was that? Of course the man burned women. He had a much-publicised trail of ashes in his wake to prove it.

'Badly,' he murmured, his voice tinged with regret. 'Hence my rules.'

Throat swollen, she had to squeeze out the words. 'What rules are they, Finn?'

'No commitment. No emotional ties. Just pleasure beyond your wildest imagination.'

'That sounds...'

'*Good.* It's good, baby. For as long as it lasts. A few hours at the most. Then there's nothing but emptiness. So believe me when I say keep safe and don't be lured by your inner fire. Especially when it ignites for me.'

A ten-bell siren blared through her head, silenced her desire. He was only being brutally honest. No flippant innuendo from this man. No play on words. No clever retort. She liked the real Finn St George, she realised. Very much. He was an arrogant, seductive, sexy blend of bad-boy meets boy-next-door.

Keep safe. Good advice. Not that commitment interested her. Emotional ties made her blood run cold. She'd just lost one man she'd loved, and being obsessed with a player who rapped on death's door with alarming frequency wasn't her idea of a rollicking good time.

Still, what if Finn was the only man she'd ever want sexually? Was she crazy to want to experience such pleasure once in her life? She knew the game, the rote, had been a spectator all her life. She could play by the rules, couldn't she?

Serena fancied he could see the internal battle warring inside her, because he raised his hand and swept a strand of hair from her brow with a shiver-inducing graze.

'Trust me, beautiful. It's a bad idea.'

The main lights dimmed and what remained was a black canvas ceiling dotted with tiny pricks of light. It was like sitting beneath a million twinkling stars. So romantic that yearning pulled at her soul.

Finn eased back into his own chair, leaving her oddly bereft. Until the music struck an almighty beat and she felt the punch of power deep in the pit of her stomach. Then the full instrumental peeled from the band, the sound caroming around the vast expanse to infuse the atmosphere with what she could only describe as a seriously evocative sensual bent.

'Oh, my life.'

The thought slammed into her psyche within seconds. Finn hadn't intended bringing her here at all. So who...?

As if he could hear her mental meanderings, he murmured, 'I was coming by myself. This is a new cabaret-style show directed by a friend of mine and he sent some tickets over last night. He knows I like to blend occasionally, and they often debut in Montreal. I've no idea what to expect.'

She was pretty sure he had a better idea than she did.

'All I know is that it's strictly over eighteens and it explores human sexuality.'

Okay-dokey, then. Right up her street. *Not.*

The risqué undertone of the music was a prelude to a stage lifting from beneath the floor, bringing the performers into view, still as statues. Until the Moulin-Rouge-type beat peaked with an almighty crescendo…

The cushioned pad beneath her bottom quaked, sending a vibration straight to her core, making the hair on her arms stand on end.

And then the artists came to life.

Heat that had nothing to do with the amount of bodies packed in one space and all to do with the hedonistic bent of the performance shot through her bloodstream, growing ever hotter when the stage became a writhing mass of mind-boggling feats of flexibility and synchronicity.

Bodies were bending, stroking, touching. Hands glissaded over painted flesh, the vivid colours of their skin alive with sensuous beauty.

Hanging from the dollies above the plinth were three massive chandeliers from which acrobats were suspended, and they too began to move in a series of gyrations, spinning and twisting as they swung from one bar to another in a dizzying spectacle.

Oh. And they were all half naked. Half naked and—

She sucked in a sharp breath and Finn leaned over.

'You okay?'

'Mmm…' It came out like a groan, because where Finn had made her hot and bothered seconds before the show, now she was burning up. *The fiery one.*

'You want to leave?'

'Absolutely—' She had to take another breath as one of the female performers wrapped her legs around her partner, locked groins tight and bent backwards to the floor, as if he were sliding inside her, as if...

'Okay, let's go.'

'—not. No, I'm not leaving. I'm staying right here. A tornado whipping through the room wouldn't move me as much as this. It's... They...they're *beautiful.*'

Dancing, whirling, bending—the women were incredible acrobats, so much femininity and strength all rolled into one stunning blend.

'So strong,' she whispered in awe.

'They have to be. Strong-willed to train so gruellingly. Strong-minded to hold their positions, trust in their abilities. Believe in their talent. But elegant and graceful at the same time.'

Yes, and all the while remaining strong of heart, body and soul. No shame, only dazzling radiance.

Still staring at the stage, her mind spun. 'What are you getting at, Finn?'

'Maybe I'm just pointing out that being a woman doesn't render you weak, and being strong or unique doesn't make you less feminine.'

She didn't see all women as weak. Did she? Then again, she'd never known many women. Only her dad's bits of fluff, and they all seemed desperate somehow. Serena had watched them, thinking how bizarre they all were, flitting to and fro, trying to make her dad happy, in the idiotic assumption he would keep them. Desperate. Weak. But wholly feminine. Had she subconsciously knitted the two together?

Finn had told her she was feminine. His words, *'Of course you are... In your own unique way...'* came back to her. She'd taken them as a kind of insult, but at the same time had longed for him to mean it. Despite or perhaps because of the shoe-slipper debacle.

Finn saw far more than what met the eye. Behind the celebrity persona he had a depth of intensity and an intelligence that astounded and intrigued her.

'People underestimate you, Finn,' she murmured, and the show continued all around them, just as the world still spun, ignorant of the seismic shift inside of her.

Seismic since she suspected that he was not only right but that her issues ran far deeper. Too deep for her to delve into that gorge right now.

'Always a bad idea,' he said, with an arrogance that made her smile.

With her gaze glued to the sinuous, serpentine movements on stage, she could feel him staring at her.

'It's enthralling, don't you think?'

'Absolutely mesmerising,' he said, still watching her.

'Provocative,' she whispered.

'A unique kind of sensuality.'

Her heart did a trapeze artist flip in her chest. In Monaco he'd said similar words to her.

Unable to resist a moment longer, she turned to look at him.

Face flushed, he licked his lips, as if his mouth was over-dry.

'Finn...?' she breathed. 'Aren't you going to watch?'

'I am watching, baby. The only thing worth looking at.'

Whoosh. Her heart did another flip. Three somersaults and a free fall. And just like that she struggled to breathe.

Before she knew it her eyes had closed and she leaned forward, needing his mouth on hers so badly her entire body ached—and that was *nothing* compared to the flood of moisture low in her pelvis, the incessant clench demanding satisfaction.

French vocals drifted on the air—a sultry line that enhanced the suggestive notes pluming around them:

Would you like to sleep with me tonight?

Another Serena might have asked—a braver version, one who was confident enough to know she could satisfy a man like him, one who knew she'd feel no regrets in the morning. The real Serena couldn't guarantee any of that.

His warm breath trickled over her lips, yet intuition told her he wouldn't close the ever-so-small gap—a virtual Grand Canyon, considering the past that lay between them and all the reasons for them to rebuff this weird and wonderful attraction and simply walk away.

Just the thought that he might take the decision from her kicked her doubts to the kerb and she prised her eyes wide.

His eyes were as dark as midnight, glittering like the stars above, and from nowhere she found the strength to move in, close that gap, lick over his full bottom lip and then bite down to tease with a gentle tug.

Lust...

Finn growled.

Heat...

'Back off, Serena.'

More. Another lick. Another soft suck. Another tender bite. He returned it with sharp yet gentle teeth, then kissed away the sting, causing her to shiver and the deep ache in her body to spike.

'You really want me to take you right here?' he rasped.

That stopped her.

Visibly shaken, her hand trembled as she brushed the hair from her sticky nape and leaned back in her seat. Her sensitive breasts chafed against the cotton of her plain bra and she had to stifle a whimper.

Who knew how long she sat there, her lower body contracting around thin air, while a surge of mortification because she couldn't control her own body inched her anger levels up the charts?

Intermission hit and, unknowing what to say, what to do, feeling seven kinds of stupid that she couldn't make light of the fact that she was teetering on the edge of an orgasm or handle it in some practised feminine way, she launched to her feet.

'I'm going to the Ladies'.'

And she shot through the crowd at a fast clip.

She had to cool off and there was only one way to do it.
As far away from Finn St George as she could possibly get.

CHAPTER NINE

'Don't get a fright,' Finn murmured, taking a tentative step closer to where she stood in the dark corridor that led to the plush offices at the rear of the tent. How she'd found her way around here he wasn't sure, but for the six minutes it had taken to find her he'd never felt so ill in his life.

Seemingly ignorant of the shadows enveloping her, Serena faced the wall, her head bent forward, brow kissing the evocative red plaster, as her supple body shook violently.

His heart hammering, his insides writhing in a chaotic mess, Finn braced his hands on either side of her head, then buried his face in her neck and inhaled a sweet burst of summer fruits—a scent that pacified, a taste that he'd come to associate with her. One he would never forget. One he wanted to lap right up.

He nuzzled up to her ear. 'Let me take the edge off, baby.'

He shouldn't have brought her here. She was burning. He'd never seen anything like it. Or felt anything like it. He was going insane with lust. Yet he had no intention of taking his pleasure from her. For once in his life he was going to be unselfish. Give instead of take. Douse her fire well and good.

For a second he thought she'd refuse, and despite knowing it was probably for the best he felt his guts twist tight. And then she turned and, *bam*, her mouth was on his, and she was twining her arms around his neck and thrusting into his mouth.

Just like that his largesse slipped a gear. *Aw, man*, this was not good. This was going to be harder than he'd thought. Much, *much* harder if the erection that strained against his zipper was anything to go by.

Grateful that she'd found her way round to this section of the tent, Finn picked her up, wrapped her legs round his waist and carried her straight into his friend Zane's office, thanking fate that he'd passed the man only moments ago and orchestrated thirty minutes of privacy.

He kicked the door shut behind them and braced her against it, his lips never leaving her mouth as he rolled his hips against her heat to create the friction she needed.

His little tigress moaned and purred around his lips, thrust her hands into his hair and held on while he took her on the ride of her life.

'Finn, Finn, Finn…'

'It's okay, baby. It's okay. I'll get you over.'

'I don't like this. I've never felt like this before. It's never been this way before.'

The words poured out on a rush but he got the general gist. Sex didn't usually flip her switch. Bastard that he was, he revelled in that.

'This doesn't feel normal,' she whimpered.

'I know, beautiful.' *Nowhere near normal.*

Which was the entire problem. He was *feeling* things. Desperation, need, a want like no other. A bone-deep fervour to protect, to satisfy her every craving, her every wish, to make her come over and over until her cries of ecstasy filled his mouth. To give her the world and the stars beyond. Too much. It was all just too damn much.

Holding her up with one hand, he smoothed around her small waist, then un-popped the button of her jeans. Her piercing teased and tormented his fingers and he growled as his flesh turned to granite. *Keep it together…keep it together. What are you? A virgin?*

He wanted *in*, and the angle was all wrong, so with a light squeeze of her deliciously pert rear he loosened his hold and splayed his hand beneath the T-shirt on her back to keep her close. The touch of her fevered skin was like an electrical charge up his arm.

What he wouldn't do to have a good, *long* look at the body that had featured so prominently in his dreams. To claw at her clothes and tear her panties off with his teeth.

Serena shimmied to the floor, snatching kisses as if she never wanted to leave his mouth, and burrowed under his polo shirt, making him sweat.

Okay, then. She wasn't the patient type. Which was dangerous with a capital D because *he* was—it was the only way to stay in control.

'Slow—slow down, baby.'

She had to slow down. Before he buried himself in her dewy heat and lost himself inside her.

'Oh, God, this is so good,' she moaned.

'You knew I would be.'

'Arrogant man.'

With great pains he managed to focus on her luscious mouth and devour her, trying his hardest to focus as he slowly but surely eased the waistband of her jeans down her hips and encountered some lacy girly version of boxer shorts.

Oh, man, he was a goner. 'I have to look.'

'Now, where have I heard that before?' she panted.

Finn pulled back and ripped her hoodie and her T-shirt over her head; his temples were pounding, his blood was pounding, his erection was pounding. Everything was pounding.

Her jeans were rucked around mid-thigh, her biker boots sculpted her calves and those subtle curves were making his vision swim. Then he was seeing red... *Red?* Bra and panties. Closet girl, that was what she was.

'Red,' he growled.

His first thought was, *She's perfect*. His second thought was, *Oh, hell, she's perfect.*

Lamplight spilled over the room and he could just make out the lustrous tone of her ivory skin dusted with freckles. He wanted to lie her down and count them all, give them names and kiss every one. He wanted to crush her to him and hold on tight. And from nowhere came the senseless idea that he could be a one-woman-forever man, that she could trust him always.

With defcon speed he ruthlessly shut the notion down. He was *never* taking the risk of hurting her. He'd already done too much of that already and she didn't know half of it.

'Stop staring at me!'

'No chance.' He was looking and she was going to learn to like it, to know how seriously sexy she was.

He cursed blue to get his point across. Lots of the F-word and *gorgeous*es and *sexy*s flying out of his mouth at two hundred miles per hour.

Then he kissed her hard, to back up every word with a truckload of ardour just in case she wasn't getting the point. And with each thrust of his tongue and every swivel of his hips desire mounted, until her rapture created a cloud of erotic fervour and her rich arousal plumed in the air.

Oh, man, he wanted to bite her, mark her, brand her like the animal he was inside.

Hand splayed, he rubbed his palm over her piercing and sank it beneath her shorts, delving to touch her hot heat.

A tortured moan filled the air. His. Hers. Theirs.

She was slick and swollen with want, and when her hips bucked, moisture trickled down his finger.

'Serena…' he groaned, tormenting her with a good dose of exquisite friction.

Gingerly he peeled one shoulder strap down her upper arm, and when her perfect C's popped free the room spun as if he was on a whirly top. They were like works of art. Firm but soft. Each underswell lush and round and topped with a dusky rose nipple.

'You're so beautiful, Serena.'

Taste—he simply *had* to taste her.

Finn cupped her breast and trailed his mouth down her neck. The anticipation of reaching her tight nipple thrummed through his blood, and when he flicked his tongue over the taut peak and simultaneously pushed one finger deep inside of her, a keening cry ripped from her throat.

This was agonising. He wanted her. All of her.

Hot little pants escaped her mouth and the sight of her teeth buried in her bottom lip sent another jolt through him. When he closed his lips over her puckered flesh and sucked, the scent of her arousal filled his nostrils, making him hard enough to penetrate steel.

As if she'd lost the ability to hold her head high, Serena tipped it back to smack the wall. 'Oh. My. Life. Finn…!'

He sank his finger deeper inside her body, this time a little harder, and felt her tight walls close in, grab onto him.

He had a big problem here—a huge problem. And if he wasn't careful he would explode in his hipsters. She was so tight.

'Been a long time baby?'

'Mmm-hmm.'

She was petite to start with, and the way he was sized he would snap her in two. *Not an issue. You're not going there.* It still didn't stop him from imagining the sensation, the hedonistic pleasure, of spreading her across Zane's desk and licking her from head to foot before he plunged deep inside her slick channel.

Her hips pivoted in time to his rhythm and she grabbed his shoulders and arched her back, seeking deeper penetration.

'More?' He pushed a second finger to join the first and she spasmed around him, saying his name over and over with soft, heated, anguished cries of ecstasy.

Keep it together. Don't lose it. Don't you dare.

With one last light squeeze of her breast Finn skimmed up and over her collarbone to rub her bottom lip, back and forth. Then he pushed his index finger inside her hot moist mouth at the same time as he thrust his two fingers deep and thumbed her sweet spot to tease out her pleasure.

Plunge and stroke, here and there, until she writhed and swirled her tongue around his finger. *Holy...* And when he touched her nipple with a nice long lave of his tongue...

She *broke*, splintered, shattered, coming long and hard, spasm after spasm racking her body. The walls of her femininity closed in, squeezing his fingers as she flew apart at the seams, clamping violently in a stunning erotic symphony.

Sweat trickled down his spine, making the tight, scarred skin of his back itch. *Hold it together. Hold it.*

As she tumbled from the heights of bliss, rolling in wonder and passion and exhilaration, Finn leaned his forehead against hers, jaw locked, his total focus on willing the erection bursting out of the top of his jeans to chill out. Willing his body not to come just from watching her orgasm.

He needed air. *Now.* He was shaking from head to foot and his teeth were clamped so tight he nearly cracked a molar.

'Finn?' she breathed.

'Give me a minute.' He squeezed his eyes shut.

Her small hand slipped off his shoulder, smoothed down his chest, and didn't stop until she cupped his erection through his jeans.

He hissed out a choice curse. 'Careful, beautiful.' He placed his hand over hers to lift it to his mouth and kiss her palm. 'This can't happen between us, Serena. For starters, I haven't got a condom.' He sounded a hoarse, desperate man. Very true, that.

'It's already started, Finn.' Back down she went, fingering his jeans. 'I'm safe. You're clean, right?' She began to rip his belt buckle free.

Once more he tugged her hand away, knowing he'd never make it a third time.

'Serena, I've never had sex without a condom in my life.'

This could *not* happen. He needed a condom. It would be too close. Too intimate. Too everything.

Without a barrier he'd lose it. Lose himself. Inside her. He would mark her. Brand her. Have real trouble letting her go.

'We're stopping before we go too far.' *There. That should do it.* He sounded forceful and arrogant and domineering. And just so he could cut off the screenplay in his head he hitched up her bra strap and veiled her gorgeous breasts.

'Don't you *want* to sleep with me, Finn? Be inside me?'

He groaned long and low, never having wanted anything more in his entire life. Right now an endless reel played in his head. She was so utterly perfect for him. But he was *not* the man for her.

In another life he would think he'd finally found The One. If he'd been a different man. If he'd made different choices and hadn't caused so much pain. Pain he knew he'd eventually cause her again. He was too selfish. Unreliable.

He was also taking too long to answer, because she'd tugged her jeans into place and wriggled back into her T. All the while trying to school an expression made up of dejection and embarrassment.

'I don't do it for you, do I?'

Finn cupped her face and kissed her softly on the mouth. 'One look and you do it for me, beautiful. You always have. But, like I told you before, it's a bad idea. You'll wake up in the morning and hate me even more. Regret every minute. Feel only emptiness. It's a stone-cold feeling, Serena, I promise you.'

She stared into his eyes. 'So what was that? Friends with benefits?'

'Sure—why not? You needed me.'

'You need *me* too.' She dipped her head to where he was straining against denim and licked her lips in bashful invitation. 'At least let me...?'

Finn reared back, creating some space. *Hell, no.* If she

knelt before him, took him into her mouth, he would never get the picture out of his head.

'I won't take pleasure from you. That was for you, just this once. Never to be repeated.'

If they reached this point again he'd be powerless to stop.

The only reason he had this encounter under control was because they were in Zane's office, with no condoms, flanked by secrets and lies.

Here she was, beginning to trust him, and she couldn't. It was insane. She was forgiving him, tumbling into his arms under the influence of deceit, and he could not sink into her body, look into her eyes as he came inside her, without her knowing the full truth.

'There are many things I'm not proud of in my life. If I take from you, if I use you, it will be one too many. Do you want a friend, Serena? Or a one-night stand that leaves you frozen? We can't have both.'

For long moments she stared at her feet, drew patterns with the toe of her boot.

Then she glanced up and gave him a small, indecipherable smile. 'Then I guess…a friend.'

Finn swallowed. Hard. 'Good. Friends it is.'

Satisfied he'd taken the hard edge off his need, he grabbed her hand. 'Come hither, Miss Scott, the night is young.'

Halfway out the door she crashed to a halt, and Finn followed her line of sight to their entwined fingers, dangling between them.

Well, what do you know? He hadn't even realised. 'What's up, baby? You never held hands with someone before?'

Brow nipped, she gave a little shake of her head. 'No.'

Finn shrugged, made it easy. 'Me neither.' And before she could make more of it he hauled her out of the room. 'Now, let's get out of here. Don't know about you, but I'm starving.'

For a woman he could never have.

CHAPTER TEN

'WHAT'S GOING ON?' Serena tucked her bike helmet under one arm, shook the damp kinks out of her hair with the splayed fingers of her free hand and closed in on the small crowd gathered at the pits. 'What's the SL1 doing down here?'

One glance at her big beauty, squatting on the Silverstone circuit, looking every inch the sleek, glorious feline she was, and Serena felt her heart swell up with pride.

It wasn't until the silence stretched that she realised several pairs of peepers were soaking in the sight of her going all goo-goo—over a *car*, for heaven's sake. *Sometimes you're such a girl, Serena.*

Tearing her eyes away, she glanced up at Finn and thought, *Oh, great, here we go again.*

The early-morning sun picked out the bronze and golden tones of his hair and his deep cerulean eyes twinkled knowingly.

'Good morning, Little Miss Designer, how nice of you to roll out of bed to join us.'

His voice was deep and devastating, richly amused and lathered in sin. Then his delicious fresh scent whispered on the breeze to douse her body with scads of heat.

'While you've been getting your beauty sleep I've driven fifty laps in your pride and joy.'

Tensing, she felt the hard lip of her helmet dig into her

hip. 'I don't understand.' The only reason he would practise in her racer was if her dad had changed his mind—

Her stomach began to fizz—which was absurd. Serena knew the kind of miracle *that* would take, and she didn't think Finn had demolished every car on the fleet. Yet.

Saying that, she'd rarely seen those dark clouds of guilt overshadowing him during the two weeks since Montreal. And the thought that she'd succeeded in finagling his attention long enough for him to move on made her soul smile.

Finn swiftly dispersed the group with an arrogant jerk of his head and leaned against the car's lustrous patina. Then he crossed his arms over a delicious cerise polo shirt and ran his tongue over his supremely sensual mouth.

A mouth she shouldn't be staring at, hungering for. The problem was, her new BF had taken her to the heights of ecstasy, and every time she looked his way every blissful, shattering moment came back on a scalding rush.

Car, Serena. Focus.

'So what did you think? Of my car?' A sudden swoop of nervy fireflies initiated a frenzy behind her ribs.

'She's much like the woman who designed her. A fiery bolt of lightning.'

Okay, then. A few happiness bugs decided to join the midriff party. 'She handles well?'

'Unbe-frickin-lievebly. She pulls more G's than a space shuttle. Her curves are divine and she worships the tarmac. She's a dream, Serena. You've done an amazing job.'

The world vanished behind her eyelids as she tried to calm the internal flurry and take a breath. All the hard work, the late nights, the testing and retesting over and over, and *still* she waited for her dad to tell her she'd done well. But the admiration and respect in Finn's gaze, from a man who'd driven the greatest cars in the world, was even better.

Oh, who was she kidding? It was awesome. She felt like flying. Having a real girly moment and jumping and whooping. Which was just silly.

'Good. I'm glad.'

Finn leaned towards her and Serena was lured by his sheer magnetism. She drew forward until his husky breath tickled her ear.

'You can squeal if you want to, baby, I won't tell anyone.'

She jerked backwards. 'Don't be ridiculous.'

That fever-pitch-inducing smile widened and one solitary indentation kissed his cheek. Despicable, infuriating, *gorgeous* man.

'So how did this happen, anyway? My dad said—'

'We had it out last night. Talked long enough for him to see sense.'

From nowhere a great thick lump swelled in her throat.

Oh, honestly, he had to stop doing stuff like this. Because every time he did, another teeny slice of her heart tore free and vaulted into his hand. Serena couldn't recall the last time someone had pushed for what *she* wanted. Even Tom had tended to side with their dad.

'You'll soon learn,' he began, his voice teasing and darkly sensual, 'that it's always best to leave business down to the men, Serena.'

The blissful feeling vanished. 'You only say that stuff to pee me off.'

A devilish glint entered his eyes...

'When I tell you my condition you'll be even more so.'

'I don't like that look.' A little bit shrewd. A whole lot devious.

'You have to attend the Silverstone Ball tonight. That's the deal.'

There it went. In point five of a second. '*It*' being her stomach, hitting ground level with a sickening thud.

'No way. You know that's not my scene.'

Black-tie extravaganza to kick off the weekend of racing with VIP clientele and the usual coterie, sipping champagne, dressed up to the nines in...? No.

Just no!

'Hold up there, handsome. Your *condition*? What do you need *me* there for?'

Never mind the dresses and the shoes and the dancing and the mind-numbing chit-chat, if he thought she was suffering that soiree only to watch him portray Lothario he had another think coming!

'Your car needs to be unveiled and it's the perfect venue. You *have* to be there. This is your big moment. You need to revel in it, enjoy it. Come on, Serena, I dare you.'

'Ooh. Low, Finn, real low.' The beast knew exactly how to get a rise out of her.

Huffing out a breath, she stared unseeingly at her car while a war raged inside her. As far as big moments went this was pretty huge.

She chose her words carefully. 'On my own?'

If he was taking a woman she wanted to know so she could prepare herself. It was crucifying, waiting for him to choose a new starlet.

True, she'd been batting away the sneaking suspicion that he'd already done so for days. What with the odd phone calls he refused to answer in front of her. The ones that made his jaw set to granite as his gaze locked on the screen before he glanced at her with something close to remorse.

If not a woman, who else?

Then again, she doubted he'd had the time to wield his charm elsewhere. More often than not they were together. Which brought on a whole new set of problems. Because while she liked having him as a friend—a pretty cool friend, as it turned out, who'd sneaked her into the premiere of the latest action flick last night—it was getting harder and harder to keep her hands off him.

All in all, since Montreal her sanity was slowly being fed through a shredder.

'You'll hardly be on your own, Serena. The entire team is going and you'll be walking in there with me.' He gave her a wink that made her feel dizzy. 'I get first dance.'

Oh. Well, then. Those fireflies started doing an Irish jig. He was taking *her*, not some flashy starlet. He was going to dance with *her*, not the latest paddock beauty. As friends, of course. Unless he'd changed his mind...

Suddenly *her* mind made the oddest leap, to a vision of her biker leathers, and a groan ripped from her chest. 'And what exactly would I *wear*?'

He chuckled at that. Actually laughed.

'What's funny?'

'And she says she's not a woman.'

Serena threw him a few daggers, wholly unamused.

'Don't worry, okay?' A smile seeped through his voice. 'We'll find something.'

'*We?* Are you worried I'll turn up in T-shirt and jeans and embarrass you?'

Fully expecting some wisecrack, she was unprepared for the way he reached up and tenderly brushed a lock of damp hair from her brow. Only to melt when he stroked down her cheek with the side of his index finger.

'Listen to me. I would dance all night with you wearing a driver's suit—I wouldn't change you for the world. But what I *don't* want is for you to feel uncomfortable or out of place. Why don't you think of it as an adventure? If you have the time of your life, that's great. If you don't, nothing lost. At least you'll have tried. For you. And you'll have given the SL1 the launch she deserves. Come on, it'll be fun.'

The only thing she heard were his words *I wouldn't change you for the world.* And she knew he meant every single one.

'Know what I tell every rookie when he faces the fast lane? Fear is a choice. Don't choose it, Serena.'

In some sort of Finn-induced trance, she murmured, 'Okay.'

She could do this. Launch her car. Dance with Finn. Keep it friendly.

If he still wanted that. She wasn't so sure any more. In

truth she had no idea why they were still fighting it. *Stone-cold morning-after, full of regrets about being one of many.*

'Good.' He delved into his pocket and whipped out his mobile. 'I'll go make some calls and we'll head back to the Country Club. Within two hours you'll have half a boutique in your suite.'

Another wink as he backed towards the garage and her insides went gooey.

'Trust me, baby.'

Trust him.

Why did he always say that? Because he wanted her to trust him so badly? Or was he transmitting some kind of subconscious warning that she shouldn't? The problem was, his warnings were now falling on deaf ears.

Especially since his predicted 'stone-cold emptiness' had evolved regardless. Wherever they went, whatever they did, when the time came to part, stone-cold was exactly what she felt—right down to her bones.

Until her sheets twisted with hot longing and her mind saw an evocative cabaret with her and Finn centre stage. Her only thought: *I want that man. I always have and I'm going to have him.*

To hell with it all.

It was becoming harder and harder to control that voice, to silence the woman inside.

Serena ambled across the tarmac towards the perimeter, enticed by the serenity of lush green meadows—an endless landscape of possibilities. She struggled to remember if she'd ever seen her life that way. As an adventure. Always the pragmatist, she'd never been a dreamer.

There was Finn, with his rich and wondrous, albeit debauched past, but at least he'd lived life to the full. While she'd been fighting that voice, the woman she was inside, since she was thirteen years old, having just rolled onto her stomach in bed, only to wince as the sensitive mounds of flesh on her chest crushed against the mattress. Then a few days later the stomach pain had come, to signal an even bigger humiliation—how to buy panty liners surrounded by men. And that had been nothing on the hormonal avalanche making her feel confused, wishing more than ever that she had a mum of her own. She'd been lost—like a stranger in her own skin. Trapped in someone else's body.

Looking back, it was all so clear to her now. Raised a tomboy, she'd hastened to repress her nature. Yet slowly, secretly, she'd begun harbouring fantasies of more. Dreaming. Easily beguiled by a man who'd lured her with lies and deceit, making the temptation to be all things feminine a compulsion she couldn't resist.

Tipping her face skyward, she let the sun warm her face and breathed through the hurt in her heart. The sinister backlash would stay with her always.

Ever since Finn had made her realise she saw women as weak the idea had rubbed her raw, like a scratch to her psyche.

The naked truth? She was petrified of being a woman. It led her to make bad choices. To walk headlong into betrayal. Pain. Weakness. It led her to lack-lustre sexual encounters as her body fought her will.

So here she was. Twenty-six years old. Still trapped.

Until Finn touched her and she threatened to burst out of her own skin.

Serena knew it was foolhardy but she wanted a good long look at the woman beneath. The person she'd stifled and ignored. And she trusted him.

Fear is a choice.

So hours later, when rails upon rails of dresses in every shape and hue lined her rooms, she duelled with the bouts of anxiety and doubt and managed to conquer each and every one.

For years she'd vowed that her past would not define her. Yet it had. All along. Well, no more.

A strong woman would pursue what she desired. If Finn

was prowling for some female company to take to his bed tonight Serena wanted to be it.

They could still be friends afterwards. She'd just have to prove it to him.

'I'm in the cocktail bar. Come for me?'

Finn strolled into the bar of the swanky Country Club and made a quick sweep of the softly lit circular lounge.

Designed in a sinuous art nouveau style, the architecture was a showcase for curvy lines where no shadows could lurk and deep furniture made from exotic woods, lending a warmth that pervaded his bones. A warmth that grew hotter as his eyes snagged on his prey, her back facing him, perched on a high stool at a central island bar made of iridescent glass.

Whoosh. His blood surged through his veins, drowning out a soft croon.

For one, two, three beats he stared. Because something was different and he certainty had faltered. Then she leaned towards the barman as if she hung on his every word…tipped her head back with infectious laughter and graced him with her exquisite profile.

'Holy…'

Confidence. She was incandescent with it.

His heart cramped, stopped and started again, as if he were crashed out on a gurney in need of some chest paddle action.

Commanding his feet to move, he ordered himself to be calm—not to pick her up, twirl her around the floor, tell her she looked every inch the stunning beauty she was. Not to kiss her hard on the mouth before taking her upstairs to slake this crazy lust and devour her gorgeous body for days.

Instead he scoured his mind for an appropriate Finn St George comment that would do the job whilst ensuring they slept between separate sheets—because his control was as treacherous as an oil slick.

This thing, this friendship between them, was taking on a dangerous bent, and losing the precarious hold on his sanity wouldn't be pretty.

The dilemma being, he couldn't disengage himself from her heavenly pull.

When the moon rose so too did his demons, and there he lay, tormented, although adamant that his endless procrastinating would cease with the rising sun. Then she appeared, all fire and dazzle, with her snarky wit and her beautiful smile, dragging him from the darkness into the light more magnificently than any sunrise could ever do. Leaving him torn asunder once more, frustrated and infuriated with the ugly little corner he'd found himself in.

Keeping her in the dark had been an easy enough decision to make after Singapore, when he'd still been able to taste the metallic tang of blood and they hadn't been face-to-face. All black and white, his reasoning had been crystal clear. Protect her at all costs. No harm done.

But as one day had overtaken another *simple* had accelerated to *beyond complicated.*

Now Finn was loath to tamper with her contentment, to substitute the happiness in her eyes with hate and betrayal. At the same time he was selfish enough to want her to look at him that way a while longer. As if he was a good man. As if he *hadn't* led her brother to his death. As if his day of reckoning *wasn't* hurtling towards him.

Before he even reached her side she stilled. Curled her fingers around the beaded purse on the glass bar-top. Closed her eyes and just…breathed.

Honest to God, what they did to each other defied logic. It was a car bomb waiting to detonate if he didn't defuse it somehow.

Gripping the back rail of her stool, he became enraptured by her fiery river of hair—the way the sides were loosely pinned back to create a cascade of soft, decadent curls down her back.

Thought fled and he dipped his head to kiss her bare shoulder. But he slammed on the brakes in the nick of time, making do with a long, deep inhale. In place of her usual fruity undertones there was an evocative note of something dark and distinctly passionate, reminiscent of her arousal.

His body quaked as that scent registered in his brain like a Class A narcotic and he growled in her ear, 'Looking good, baby.'

A slight tremble passed over her before she swivelled on her bottom and slipped off the stool. Then he got a really good look, and his heart started doing that palpitation thing again. *Wow*, she was filling out. That over-thin look of Monaco was being replaced with subtle curves.

Her pewter dress was snug, held up by one heavily beaded shoulder strap which trailed down the side of a boned bodice, cupping her breasts, moving down to a small bustle at her hip. Her skirts were frothily layered, plunging to the floor in swathes of a lighter toned silver, the hue turning darker by degrees to charcoal and finally edged in ebony. It was a sexy version of rock-chick princess, with Serena lending it her own unique kick.

He was left with the ludicrous urge to lift the froth and take a peek at her feet.

A small smile teased her lips. 'Don't tell me. You need to look.'

Finn shrugged, feeling oddly boyish. He'd never been obsessed with a woman, and the hunch that obsession was definitely the evil he was up against made him recoil, take a step back.

Serena, however, took that as an invitation to show off, and she slowly, seductively, inched her skirts up her calves, then lifted her dainty little foot and flexed her ankle this way and that.

The diamond-studded sandals twinkled in the light, sending prisms of colour to dance across the walnut floor.

'You're very pleased with yourself, there, Miss Scott.'

Smoky sultry make-up enhanced the colour of her grey gaze as she sparkled up at him. Lips glossed, pink and full taunted him as she spoke in a rush. 'I am. No boots, no slippers, and I can actually walk. Who knew wedge sandals actually existed?'

The way she was looking at him—confident, serene, enchanting...

Dammit. How was he going to get through this night? Need was a ferocious claw in his gut, slicing deeper with every second.

'You look sensational, baby.'

'Why, thank you, Finn. But do you know what's really scary?'

'What?'

Her brow nipped, as if she were controlling her emotions. 'I think I do too.'

'That's my girl.' His voice cracked under pressure. 'Let's get this show on the road. The helicopter awaits.' He held out his arm and shut down every possessive instinct in his body. 'Shall we go to the ball, Miss Scott?'

She slipped under the crook of his arm, pressed her breast in tight to his side and his pulse shot through the roof.

'Why, yes, I believe we shall, Mr St George. I have a feeling this is going to be a night to remember.'

Finn tried to swallow around a lifetime of regrets. 'Curiously enough, so do I.'

CHAPTER ELEVEN

'CONGRATULATIONS, SERENA, she's a beauty.'

'Thanks!' she said for the hundredth time as she cut through the swathe of racing drivers, TV pundits and VIP celebrities littering the champagne reception.

Despite her stomach doing a really good impression of a cocktail shaker, she'd slipped free of Finn's arm an hour earlier. Half of her was adamant not to appear clingy and her other half was determined to venture out on her own. An endeavour that had whipped her into a whirlwind of team chit-chat, photos and promo for the SL1 until she felt high as a proverbial kite.

It couldn't possibly be the champagne. Truthfully, she thought it was a disgusting blend of wince-worthy tartness and bubbles exploding up her nose. She'd do anything for a beer.

Spotting a familiar face in a bunch of footballers, she pulled up alongside her dad, waited for a lull and then tugged at his sleeve. 'Have you seen Finn anywhere? We're supposed to be heading into the marquee for dinner.'

'Not lately. Good God, you look stunning, sweetheart. I had to pick my jaw up off the floor when you walked in.'

'That makes two of us.' Jake Morgan sidled up to join them, his chocolate gaze liquid with warmth. 'You look fantastic, Serena.'

'Oh, stop, now you're making me blush.' She gave a small

smile to soften the brush-off—she still wasn't used to compliments. She kept expecting someone to shout *Impostor! Fraud!* Even if she felt…well, beautiful for the first time in her life. All giddy and girly.

And if that aroused an anxious tremble in her stomach she ignored it. There'd be no dark shadows tonight.

She took a deep, fortifying breath and switched gears. 'I can't wait to see my baby whizz around Silverstone tomorrow.'

'She'll win for sure,' someone said.

'Too right she will.' *As long as Finn kept his mind on the game.*

'Can I get you a drink before we head over?' Jake asked.

Inwardly cringing at the thought that she'd end up with another glass of fizz, she said, 'Actually, Jake, I'll come with you.'

The bar was the traditional mahogany type: deep and framed with brass rails. Serena gripped the cold metal as they deliberated over the mirrored wall of various optics.

'What does gin taste like?' she mused.

'Not sure, but it used to put my mother in a crying jag.'

Serena snorted a laugh, turned round. 'Really?'

And *that* was when she caught a glimpse of dirty blond hair in the mirror's reflection and twisted to see Finn laughing in that charming, charismatic way of his.

'You pick, Jake. I'll be back in a tick.'

Off she went, diving through the throng and popping out at the 'Finn cluster' planted at the top of some stone steps leading to the vast lawn—a lush green blanket saturated with an array of iconic racing cars from past to present, as well as supercars, helicopters and yachts in a huge luxury showcase.

As if Finn sensed her behind him he reached round, grabbed for her hand, then pulled her into the fray and introduced her with practised ease and a pulse-thrumming smile. A smile she tried to emulate as he assaulted her senses, rubbing his thumb over the ball of her hand, making her bones liquefy and then leaning in until his dark scent fired heat through her veins.

'You enjoying yourself?'

'Yeah, I am. Surprise!' she said, only to cringe at the quiver in her voice, musing that she might be a league too deep with this man who effortlessly consumed her. 'Are you coming in for dinner? We're being seated any minute.'

'We?'

'Jake is at the bar, ordering drinks. He's waiting for me.'

Finn glanced towards that very spot, staring with an enigmatic hardness that turned pensive. Then he squeezed her hand until she flinched. *What the—?*

Jerkily he released her. 'Sorry, beautiful.'

If she didn't know better she would think he'd shocked himself.

'Sure, I'll follow. You go ahead,' he said, with an austere jerk of his head and a dark note to his drawl that she couldn't grasp.

As it was, they were halfway through their appetizers when he finally deigned to join the highly sophisticated mix, whipping out all the weapons in his loaded arsenal to schmooze his tardiness away.

And while every man and woman fell beneath his spell Serena stared at those tight shoulders, filling out his suave custom-made tux, and fought with disquiet. He appeared ruffled. As if he'd been thrusting his fingers through his hair. Or someone else had. *Stop. Just stop. You're being ridiculous.*

Soon, she told herself. As soon as the first band came on he would come for her to dance. Although the anticipation was a killer. Especially when she could feel his eyes burning into her flesh when he thought she wasn't looking.

What he failed to grasp was that her every sense was attuned to his high frequency. Every word from his lips dusted over her skin like the petals of the wild orchids that trailed from the crystal centrepiece, and every deep, sinful chuckle tightened the flesh between her legs. The waiting, waiting, slowly drove her insane, until at one point his gaze was so intense a tornado whipping through the room couldn't have stopped her meeting it across the table.

Finn placed his palm on his chest, as if his heart ached, and, *oh*, her own thumped in response. But then he pulled his phone from the breast pocket and she realised it must have been on vibrate. *Idiot.*

Her stomach hit the velvet seat with a disheartened thump even as she tensed with the chill of suspense.

Much as he had on another few occasions, he stared at the screen, then glanced back up, his demeanour fierce, indecipherable, his jaw locked tight, something dark and portentous swirling in his eyes.

Guilt. Another woman. It had to be.

Throat thick, she had to swallow hard. 'Aren't you going to answer it?'

It was the same question she'd previously voiced, and for the first time she *wanted* him to say no. Not to spoil the moment. Their night.

Except this time he stood. 'Yes. I've been waiting for a call. It's…important.'

'Is that right?' She sounded snarky, but right now she couldn't care.

One of the black-and-white-garbed waiters lowered a gold-trimmed plate in front of her and the sweet aroma of salmon and asparagus hit her stomach like battery acid even as she told herself she could be leaping to conclusions. But why act so guilty if it was innocent? Either way, she had no right to be upset, no claim on him whatsoever. *Exactly.* She was not furiously jealous. Absolutely not. That would mean she was far more emotionally involved with him than good sense allowed.

'I'll be back in a while.'

Mutely she nodded. Forty minutes later she was still calling herself fifty kinds of fool. He'd left. He must have. And while an orchestra of pain and hurt struck a beat inside—

directed at herself for believing she had a shot with him—she refused to let him take her pride from her tonight.

The bolt of fortitude was like taking a match to gasoline, and fury hit her in an explosion of fire. Once again she'd set herself up for a fall. But she wasn't going down. Not this time.

'Serena? The band is striking up. Would you do me the honour?'

Glancing up to Jake's handsome face, she felt her throat pulse, raw and scratchy. Was she seriously going to sit here all night like a fool, waiting for a man who might never come back? Was she really that desperate?

'Sure, Jake,' she said, ignoring the forlorn thump behind her breast telling her that this felt very, very wrong. 'That'd be great.'

It was like being confronted with his nemesis. The antithesis of everything he was.

Guts writhing in a chaotic mess, Finn leaned against the wall at the rear of the dimly lit ballroom, thinking how poignant it was to be enveloped by shadows—everything Serena feared—as he watched Jake Morgan enfold her hand and beckon her to the dance floor.

His body jerked on a visceral instinct to go over there, stop the other man from taking her in his arms. But, dammit, he could be honourable for once in his life. Step aside. Let the guy make his move. It was a thought he'd battled with all night. Would have surrendered to if it weren't for the undesirable, inexplicable, violent primal instincts that demanded he protect her. Possess her. Take her. Make her his.

But Finn knew the fall out from such selfishness. It had chased his career, fed off the high-octane rush of success, abandoned his mother when she'd needed him, left Eva to the heart-wrenching fate of watching her die. It had cost this woman her brother. So this, he assured himself, was an argument he would win. He wanted her to be happy.

One of the country's top bands struck out with a Rat-Pack number and when Serena offered Jake a small smile and moved into his embrace, white-hot lightning shot up his forearms, tearing through muscle. He had to shake his fists loose. What was wrong with him? He had to get a grip.

Jake was a good guy. Reliable. Honourable. Chances were *he* could remember the names of every woman he'd slept with.

Jake was trustworthy. What was more he hadn't just ended a call to the Chief of the Singapore Police, who'd discovered a new lead and was about to make an arrest.

Insides shaking, he blanked his mind. *Back away, Finn. Back the hell away.*

She could have a relationship with this guy. Finn knew nothing about those apart from the fact that the mere word spawned ramifications that were bad for his respiratory rate.

Across the room Jake fitted his hand to Serena's dainty waist, tugged her close, whispered in her ear, and Finn felt the first fissure *crack* in his sanity. His every possessive, protective instinct kicked and clawed with steel-tipped talons, tearing his insides to shreds, until he was back in that cell, fists balled, ready to protect what was his. And had it worked? No!

The dark licked around the edges of his life.

'Finn?'

Sweat trickled down his spine, making the skin on his back itch as violence poured through his veins. He'd been a stranger to brutality before Singapore and now, like then, it coated his tongue with vile bitterness.

Pain shot up his temples.

'Finn? You okay, my man?'

Michael Scott.

'Gotta go,' Finn said. 'Something's come up. Can you tell Serena…?'

Any response was lost as he shoved through the dou-

ble doors, commanding his body to stay in control before
darkness engulfed him and his demons wreaked havoc on
his soul.

Serena waltzed across the marble foyer of the Country Club
as if her squished feet *weren't* throbbing and her legs *didn't*
feel as if they'd been chewed by a Doberman.

Heart weary, her only thought a hot bath and some sleep,
she rode the elevator to the top floor, then slipped through
the yawning metal doors—and stumbled to a halt.

A maid shuffled on her feet outside Finn's suite, biting
on a torn fingernail.

Unease coiled through Serena's midriff. 'Is there a problem?'

The brunette jerked upright, wide-eyed. 'I…I'm sorry,
Miss Scott, I heard a crash as I was passing so I knocked to
check everything was all right.' She gave a tremulous smile.
'He isn't answering. You're with Mr St George, yes?'

Serena frowned, then realised the maid must have seen
her in his suite earlier, put two and two together and came
up with six.

A crash? Oh, God. What if he was hurt? Had had some
kind of accident?

Chin up, she lied through her teeth. 'Yes, we're together.
Don't worry—I'm sure everything is fine. But, while
you're here, I've lost my room card. Could you switch me
in, please?'

Antsy, suddenly slapped with the suspicion that he could
be having sex in there—which would seriously be one humiliation too many—Serena tap-tap-tapped one diamanté
toe on the floor.

As soon as the maid dipped into a curtsey and turned to
walk away Serena slipped into the room. A room filled with
dark shadows. She blinked rapidly to adjust her vision and
when the scene crystallised, she sucked in air at the sight
before her. One surely from her nightmares.

Trashed. His room was completely and utterly trashed.

Clothes were strewn all over the floor, as if his luggage had been overturned from the stand. A floor lamp was lying drunkenly on one side and the bed was stripped; dark silver satin pouring over the sides. The notion that he'd just had frenzied sex all over them crushed her heart.

It wasn't until she spotted the man himself, hands braced on the curved walnut bar, head bowed, white dress shirt damp and clinging to his back, that a portentous sensation crept up her arms. This didn't look like a seduction scene. It looked like—

'Oh, my God, Finn, has your room been ransacked? You have to call Security!'

Spotting the phone on the bedside table, she dashed over to call Reception.

'You know,' he said easily, 'that would be a very good idea. Perhaps they could take me away and lock me up.'

Reaching for the phone, her hand froze in mid-air. '*You* did this?'

She took his silence as a yes and shivered right down to her toes.

The atmosphere had turned thick with danger. She could virtually *feel* his darkness, blacker than ever before. And the urge to turn, to leave, was so strong she had to push her feet to the floor until they rooted—she would *never* be frightened of this man.

'But why?'

'Get out, Serena. Now. Before I break.'

Break? What was he talking about?

He swiped a bottle of tequila from the marble bar-top and poured the liquid into a crystal tumbler.

'Finn?' she said, panicking as he raised the glass to his lips and took a long swallow. 'What are you doing? You're driving tomorrow!'

'Nagging, Miss Scott? Now, that is a typical female trait.

One unbelievably hot dress and you're halfway there already.'

'You were the one who dressed me up! Only to disappear on a booty call and leave me there.'

A humourless laugh broke past his lips. 'A booty call? Is that what you thought?'

'What else was I supposed to think?'

With a severe kind of control, completely at odds with the state of the room, he turned to face her and air hit the back of her throat. His beautiful blue eyes were black with guilt, devastation and fury. So much fury it poured off him in waves. Great tidal waves of anguish.

'Hold up there, Lothario. What are you angry with *me* for?'

Slam went the glass to the marble and liquid sloshed over the crystal rim. 'No booty call. But it didn't take *you* long to fall into the arms of another man, did it?'

Serena flinched at the scathing lash of his tongue, the cut biting deep.

She'd messed up. Royally.

Raising one arm, Finn pointed due west and emotion gushed on a voice thick and unsteady. 'Do you have *any* idea how hard that was for me? To see his arms around you, holding you close? To walk away thinking you were better off with him?!'

Words blasted from him like bullets—*bang, bang*—until she rocked where she stood. Then she cursed for thinking the worst of him.

'I'm sorry. I waited and he asked me to dance. That's all we did—dance. I…' Her heart was beating so hard and loud she could barely think. But never mind her pride. She owed him this much. 'I only want you, Finn.'

Serena held her breath, waited. She didn't think it was possible for him to look even more tortured, but he did.

'You have to leave.' He stabbed his fingers through his

damp hair, then pawed down his face. 'Please, Serena, just go. I don't know how long I can hold on.'

Realisation hit and her entire world narrowed to this point. This man. 'So don't. Let go.'

Though her insides trembled, she commanded her feet to move deeper into the shadows and reached up to grip the zipper hook at the side of her dress. Slowly she tugged downward.

Fists clenching, he shook his head. 'Stop. Just stop. I'm on the edge here, Serena, and I can't control myself with you. I don't think you'll like that.'

As if he'd tossed her into a bramble bush, her skin prickled all over with the flash replay of violent hands gripping her throat, twisting her wrists, pinning her down—

No. *No!* This man was Finn. Granted, she'd never seen him so dark before, and it made her wonder if she was missing something, but still… 'I can handle it. I can handle you. I'm stronger than that, Finn.' Clearly he lacked faith in himself but she trusted him. Completely. Utterly.

She dragged the single beaded shoulder strap down her arm and teased the satin past her plunge bra to her waist.

His throat convulsed. 'Don't you dare, Serena. Don't you *dare.*'

She hurled his words from the yacht in Monaco so long ago back at him, amazed at how far they'd come, how far they'd travelled. 'Oh, Finn, you should know better than to challenge me. Especially in that gorgeous husky voice of yours.'

Shimmying, she eased the rucked material past her hips and the pewter satin rustled to the floor to pool at her feet. Leaving her standing in a black plunge bra, tiny lace panties and studded heels. Now, if she could just breathe she might get through this.

With his shirt agape, she could see his chest heave and the way he looked at her—with such heat. Such fierce desire and molten need.

A look so hot she melted beneath his gaze, pooling like gasoline, brandishing her earthy colours. Raw, elemental and utterly flammable.

'Serena,' he growled. 'I'm hanging on by a thread here, baby girl.'

'You know what, Finn? I love it when you call me that.' To think this man could have any women in the world and yet wanted her intimately, with such desperation, made her feel invincible. Confident. Beautiful. A real woman for the first time in her life.

He pointed at the door. 'You've got three seconds to run. Three.'

Up came her chin as she walked towards him with a sway in her hips she'd never before possessed, and then she pressed her hand to his hot flesh, felt the rapid thump of his heart beneath her palm.

'Two,' he bit out. Sweat glimmered on his skin and his broad shoulders quaked as he fought the immense power of his body. 'I can't promise I won't hurt you.'

'I *know* you won't.'

No more waiting. Avoiding. If this signalled the end of them, the end of their friendship, so be it. She didn't want another friend. She wanted a lover—the only man she'd ever truly desired.

'The fight is over, Finn.'

'One,' he said fiercely. 'You're making the biggest mistake of your life here, baby.'

'Then so be it.'

Snap.

CHAPTER TWELVE

FAST AND FRENZIED, as if he were lost beneath an unseen power, entranced by a dark, feral spell, Finn simultaneously crashed his mouth over hers, gripped the front fastening of her bra and tore it wide.

'Skin,' he commanded around her mouth as he tugged the straps down her arms and tossed the black scrap across the room. 'I want nothing between us.'

'Whatever you want.' Her voice was as shaky as the rest of her and for a second her inner voice whispered that she was mad. Totally out of her league. With no idea of how to give such an intensely passionate man what he needed.

Following her instincts, she placed her hands on his honed chest, then swept them up and over his shoulders, taking his shirt with her until it bunched and locked around his thick upper arms.

Finn shucked it off the rest of the way and grappled with the fastening at the front of his waist.

She'd never seen him like this. Ever. No practised seduction. He was uncoordinated. Lost. And to think she was the inducement made her blood surge with elation and fear and an excitement so intense she ached with it.

A sharp hiss whistled through his teeth as he fought with his tuxedo trousers and she simultaneously pushed his hands away and broke their lip-lock. 'Let me do it.'

Not easy when he sank his hands into the fall of her hair,

tilted his head and crushed his lips over hers, banishing
every thought from her brain. He ravished her with a kiss
that was desperate and messy but she loved it. Loved the
way he thrust his tongue into her mouth and groaned with
need and contentment. A sound of soul-wrenching solace.

Now she was the one who fumbled with the rotten button.
Heavens, he was bursting past the satin waistband, and when
she thumbed the velvet head of his erection and encountered
slick moisture her knees refashioned themselves into rubber.

A deep groan rumbled up his chest and he simply…tore
the trousers off, buttons pinging, material shredding—the
sounds of patience evaporating in the sultry air.

Then his long, thick length was in her hand and she
couldn't even close her fingers around it. *Oh, my life.* She
stroked up and down his erection as best she could and a
sharp tug at the base of her abdomen made her insides clench.
It felt as if she was contracting around thin air.

'Finn,' she whimpered. 'I need you inside me so bad.'

With an agonised moan, he jerked from her grasp. 'Soon.
We need to slow this down or it will be over before it's even
started.'

A sob of frustrated need broke from her throat. 'Finn,
please.'

'That's it. Say my name. Tell me you want this. Want me.'

'I do. I do.' A wave of dizziness hit her and when she realised she wasn't breathing she gasped in air.

He nuzzled deliciously across her jaw, scraped her neck
with his teeth, and somehow she knew exactly what he
wanted.

'Go ahead—do it,' she demanded, frantic for his mark,
and he sucked on her skin until her eyes rolled into the back
of her head. She had to clutch his wide shoulders to stop dissolving in a puddle at his feet.

Beneath her palms she felt his tight muscles relax, as
if he was slowly relinquishing the image of someone else
and staking his claim on her. Branding her. And she loved

it. Loved his sublime body too. From the lean ridges of his washboard abs to his sculpted arms—arms that made her feel gloriously safe, protected, coveted. Girly needs, but she was too far gone to care. She was tired of fighting them, weary of the constant struggle to stay strong. She only wanted him to hold her tight. For just a little while.

'You're so beautiful, Serena.'

Wherever his lips touched his urgent breath left heat—all the way down to her breast, where his hand cupped, where his thumb brushed over her tight nipple.

Her flesh ached for more, puckering when he took it into his mouth to swirl it and tongue it and suck it in a way she felt deep inside her pelvis.

She started to cry out but his mouth came right back, covered hers again, his fierce kiss silencing her until she surrendered to the sheer bliss of it all.

Finn splayed his hand over her stomach, rubbed her piercing with his palm, and his erection jerked against her bare thigh. Oh, that definitely did it for him. She wondered, then, what he'd think of the base of her spine...

'As divine as these panties are,' he said hoarsely, wrapping his fingers around the lace, 'you're even more so.' And he tore them clean off.

'*Ohh*, my life.'

Then he cupped her intimately, possessively, wickedly. 'Wet...*sooo* unbelievably wet and hot.'

The deep rasp of his voice, the seductive touch of his fingers against her slick and swollen folds, made her move to create the friction she craved, and within seconds her knees gave out.

'I've got you, baby.' Curving his arm around her waist to hold her upright, he thrust a finger inside her.

'Finn... Finn.' Needing his lips back on hers, his taste on her tongue, she pushed into his mouth with a boldness she'd never before dared, mimicking what he was doing with his hand as she rode his finger to completion.

The vibrations gathered force like a flock of birds sprouting wings and flying up into the sky, taking her with them far up and away as her body flew apart at the seams.

Flailing, she clutched his tight shoulders—shoulders that shifted in a delicious pattern as he gently tumbled her atop the bed.

Shivering, tingling with aftershocks, she writhed on the cool satin as he crawled over her.

'*Aw, man*, you are so incredibly, amazingly perfect. You drive me crazy, Serena. From the first moment I saw you I wanted you in my hands.'

Those very hands were shaking, but no more than hers, as he stroked up her waist and teased her ripe nipples in an unrelenting current of pleasure.

'You...you did?' Arching her back, she silently pleaded, then opened her legs wide to coax him into settling between her thighs.

He did too. Lowering his delicious weight until she could feel his hardness where she wanted him most.

'Oh, yeah. And know what else?'

'What?'

'I wanted to know how you would taste. Not only here...' He laved her nipple and gently sucked the peak into his mouth, stoking the internal fires he'd just doused. Then he shifted further down, gave the silver loop a quick lick. 'And here...' Another shift. 'But especially...here.'

Before she even knew what he was about he was at the juncture of her thighs and taking a long, leisurely cat-like lick up her still swollen folds, which still beat a tattoo of lingering pleasure. She couldn't possibly...

Serena bucked off the bed. Okay, this was really new to her, and she wasn't so sure, and it was a raw, open feeling.

'Finn?' she breathed, with vulnerability lacing her voice, making it almost inaudible.

'You taste so good, baby. I'll never get enough of you.'

Oh. His words were intoxicating, making her feel giddy,

making her heart soar. Which was just silly—she knew full well she needed to keep her heart out of this.

'Trust me. Relax. You'll love it.' He trailed lush, moist kisses across her inner thighs and she could feel his hot breath dusting her flesh. 'Heaven. I'm in sweet, delicious heaven. I love how good you taste. I knew you would.'

Gently, he sucked her clit into his mouth, pushed his tongue inside her, and every rational thought evaporated as he devoured her body and mind.

Within seconds she was writhing, fisting the trillion-count sheets. 'Finn! I can't take much more.'

'I want you mindless. Desperate. Needing me as much as I need you.' His gasped words were threaded with a hint of delicious agony. 'Able to take all of me.'

'Finn, please. I'm going out of my mind here. I'll do anything. Just give it to me, for heaven's sake—'

With a primitive sound that rumbled from his chest he crawled back up her body, prowling like a starved animal, his eyes dark as midnight, his body shaking with the strain of holding back.

'Anything?'

'Anything,' she said, softly panting, her gaze fastened on his delectable mouth.

'Beg me for it.'

Time stilled together with her heartbeat.

Power play. Control, she realised. Dominance. Her effect on him scared him. Made him feel out of control. And he wanted it back.

Yet how many times had *she* felt that way? Vulnerable, desperate to regain command of her life after the attack.

With no hesitation she reached up, cupped his gorgeous face, brought his mouth down to hers and kissed and begged and pleaded, told him exactly what she wanted him to do, using every uncouth word she could think of, until his eyes sparked electric blue and the arms that braced either side of her were shaking. And then—*thank you, God*—he thrust inside her in one powerful lunge, filling her huge and hard, covering her body with his, his possession so total she ceased breathing.

'Bliss. Sheer…bliss.'

Her lashes fluttered downward as his solid flesh pulsed inside her, making her feel exquisitely stretched. He felt *shockingly* good.

Pausing, perhaps as stunned as she was, he held still, his lips against the throbbing vein in her neck where he inhaled deeply.

A sharp arrow of unease burst through the rapture. 'Finn…?'

'Shhh, baby. I'm listening to your heartbeat, deep and hard and true. I'm soaking in your scent, rich with your arousal for *me*. Knowing…'

'Knowing?' she whispered.

'This is the closest I'll ever get to heaven.'

Oh. Her heart filled to bursting for him.

Serena sank her fingers into his damp hair and held him tightly to her. All the while fighting a punch of panic. This shouldn't be so intimate.

A chord of vulnerability sang to her heart and she squeezed her eyes shut. She didn't understand any of this. Not her body's reaction to him nor the emotions swirling inside her.

Finn finally raised his head and began to move tentatively. 'Look at me,' he ordered.

Serena opened her eyes to see him braced above her, his expression dark and fierce, so intense she trembled beneath him. Then, with their gazes locked, he began to move faster, pumping long and deep and hard, sweeping her up in a vortex of sensation so strong, so powerful, she cried out once more.

Finn captured her mouth with his—his tongue a tormenting lash of pleasure—and sank one of his hands under her bottom, lifting her, the better to meet his powerful thrusts, and grinding against her.

'Oh, *yessss*,' she moaned, raising her legs and wrapping

them around his lean hips. Her head tossed back and forth on the comforter as she fought to hold back the waves that threatened to crash over her. Almost sobbing with the fierceness of her need.

'Look at me,' he ordered again, louder this time. Heightening the sharpness of her desire. As if he didn't want her to forget who was inside her, dominating her, loving her body with his.

As if Serena could ever forget. Impossible.

She hastened to focus on his flushed face, where a thin sheen of sweat glistened on his forehead. His breath was hot and fast on her cheek; his erection throbbed inside her...then he suddenly crashed to a halt.

After a quick pause, in which he possessively gripped her waist, he pulled back. 'I want you with me when I fall. I don't want to be alone. Come with me.'

She tried, she really tried to push a *yes* past her lips, but at that moment he pushed so deep inside her that she felt him in every cell of her body and nothing came out but a high-pitched moan as she surrendered, let herself be dragged towards a climax the likes of which she'd never known.

'Finn...' she said brokenly, panicked that she wouldn't survive—that she'd die from pleasure, break after having him and losing him, shatter beneath his searing intensity.

'I know...I know.' He smoothed her damp hair back from her face. 'I'm here, baby, right here. Not going anywhere.'

She began to ride the shuddering crest. All-powerful, potent, almost violent as it ripped its way through her.

'That's it. Come for me.' He caught her small frantic cries with his mouth, tangled his tongue with hers as he upped the pace and pushed her higher than ever before.

'Finn!'

Climax was a blinding white-hot rush and she broke from his mouth as convulsions racked her body, making her spine arch violently.

Finn gave a final lunge, his dark-as-midnight eyes locked on hers, and at that moment she'd swear he touched her soul.

He stiffened, then came on a silent shudder that went on and on and on…

'Yessss…' she breathed, riveted on his gorgeous face, ravaged with pleasure, as he poured himself into her, giving her it all, and she'd never felt so strong, so powerful in all her life. She was a woman who'd just shattered this man. This beautiful, wonderful, amazing man.

A man who gave a convulsive thrust before he collapsed on top of her with a low sound of feral ecstasy. Then he wrapped her in his arms as if he never wanted to let go and nuzzled her neck, pressed a lingering kiss to the sensitive skin beneath her ear.

Serena stroked his damp hair from his brow and revelled in the feel of his body—heavy, slick and replete against hers.

Voice gruff, he murmured against her neck, 'You okay, beautiful?' with such tenderness that her chest ached.

'More than okay. That was…outrageously good.'

'Unbelievable.' He lifted his head, caught her gaze. 'Incredible.'

As if unable to stop himself he dipped his head to kiss her again—a kiss so sweet and tender that a lump pulsed in her throat and all she could think was that she didn't want to leave. She wanted to lie here forever and ever. With him.

Gently, he rolled onto his back, taking her with him, his hardness still locked inside her body, holding her tight as though fearful she would vanish into thin air.

'You'll stay here. All night. I can't let you go yet.'

'I'll stay.' Serena buried her face in his neck, tasting the musky scent of their passion and the remnants of his dark cologne. Desperately trying not to overanalyse his every touch, his every word.

He didn't do sleepovers. He'd told her that before. So maybe she was different from all the others—special enough to hold his attention. *Careful, Serena, you know better than that.* 'Yet' implied that he would let her go come morning.

Fighting the hollow emptiness in her stomach, she snuggled closer, until they clung to one another as though braced for a turbulent storm.

For now she'd just enjoy him. Take what she could. Nothing would stop her. Not even the sound of her heart cracking wide open.

Selfish. He was so selfish craving the entire night with her. No doubt he would go to hell for it. So what was new? At least he'd have tasted heaven on the way.

Self-loathing gnarled and twisted in his guts like thorny branches as the tight skin on his lower back nipped, reminding him of what lay between them. And although it was wrong to hide, he was grateful for the shadows. The only light came courtesy of the thin slice of moon shining eerily through the leaded windows, ensuring he languished in the grim certainty that his world would come crashing down with the dawn—and if this was all he had of her he was taking it. Taking it all.

Spooned into the delicate delineation of her back, with her soft skin whispering over his chest, he toyed with a lock of her ruby-red hair; corkscrewing a silken strand and watching it bounce like a loaded spring.

Aw, man, he had it bad. Knew she could steal his heart as it lay vulnerable outside his chest.

Something close to panic clutched his throat and he felt driven to lighten the mood, to lift the portentous silence, fall back on the charm that never failed to smother his emotions.

'I do find you in the most delicious compromising positions, Miss Scott,' he said, his voice a decadent purr as he kissed the graceful slope of her shoulder.

She groaned. 'Don't remind me.'

'You never did tell me why you broke into my trailer through the bathroom window four years ago.'

'I…I didn't know it was your trailer! It was identical to ours. It was pitch-black, I was tired, I'd just come back from London and my key wouldn't work.'

He trailed one fingertip down her upper arm and a quiver took hold of her svelte body, ruining the indignant tone she was aiming for. He smiled mischievously.

'Yeah, whatever. You just wanted to see me in the shower.'

'I didn't even know you!'

'Hey, no need for panty-twisting. On the scale of women trying to get my attention it veered towards the tame side. It was quite the introduction. I was the perfect gentleman too—caught you before you went splat on the floor.'

'*Gentleman*? You said my boots were the sexiest things you'd ever seen and if I wanted your body I had to leave them on!'

'Ohh, yeah! Go get them and I'll prove how serious I was.'

He'd been deadly serious—until he'd locked onto that stunning gaze of hers and his world had tipped upside down. Then his only thought had been how quickly he could shove her back out through the window and transport her to another planet. Which didn't quite explain why, at this moment, she was gloriously naked in his bed.

She coughed out an incredulous laugh. 'You're insatiable.'

'Only for you,' he said. Meaning it. She'd ruined him. No other woman in the world seemed real any more—just mere cheap imitations that might as well not exist.

Crap, he was in big trouble here. And when she canted her head and peeked up at him, brow nipped, gauging his sincerity, his stomach hollowed out.

This was getting too deep. He knew it. She knew it. He could tell by the way she turned away, scissored her legs out of the silk sheets and moved to perch on the edge of the bed.

'I should go. Let you get some sleep. You have to race in the morning and…'

And he didn't care, he realised. He would rather she stayed. Which was scarier still.

'Serena—'

That was when he saw it, in the ivory glow of the moon shimmering over her back. Artwork, moving across the base of her spine.

'Aw, baby' he growled. 'That is one hot splay of ink.'

Her spine flexed as she stiffened for a beat, then she murmured, 'Thought you might like it.'

With one touch her body softened and he traced the design with the tip of his finger, skimmed the garland of tiny pink and purple flowers outlined in black, curling into a circle to form the traditional peace symbol and then swooping outward in an elegant trail to each side of her back. But it was the small butterflies at either side, fluttering at her hip bones as if poised to fly from their captivity, that cinched his chest.

'It's beautiful, Serena.'

Intuition told him there was more to this than met the eye, but before he could pry she said, 'Finn…?' with such vulnerability that he was powerless to do anything but nuzzle closer and worship the ink with lush, moist kisses, smoothing his hands over every inch of skin he could reach, caressing her, loving her.

Until she tumbled into his arms and he made love to a woman for the very first time. Took them both soaring to the euphoric heights of nirvana, where life as he knew it ceased to exist.

When reality knocked at the temporal door of his mind Finn was half sprawled over her, one leg flung over her thighs, one arm tucked around her waist, his head cushioned on her soft breasts. Even in slumber she cradled him close, her affectionate fingers toying with and stroking his hair.

Longing nearly shattered him.

It was like coming home. An indefinable precious feeling of utter peace he wanted to wake to every morning. She felt perfect in his arms. All soft, warm woman. *His* woman.

He wasn't letting her go. He was *never* letting her go. He—

He froze. Something foreign slammed into his chest as reality hit and his life skewed dangerously.

No. No, she could never be his, he told himself, fighting the crush of what felt suspiciously like panic. Fear. He had no choice but to let her go. Watch her walk away, powerless, as her endearing affection hardened to hate.

This was what he'd been afraid of all along, he realised. Losing himself. Relinquishing his hold on the reins of his life, allowing his emotions to rule until he wanted it all. Needed a woman he could never have.

Gingerly he eased back and cool air slapped his sweat-drenched body with lucidity.

It was all for the best, right? Yes. Absolutely. He'd only cause her pain in the end, with his uncanny knack of hurting people. Eventually he'd let her down as he had Eva. He didn't trust himself not to.

Yeah, he shouldn't forget the notion that he was some kind of bad luck charm for those he cared for. Had he been able to save his mother? Tom? No. Well he'd be damned if he took Serena down too.

Curling up on her side, Serena snuggled into the pillow, subconsciously reached for him. His heart kicked with the demand to pull her into his arms. Hold her tight. Adore her. Never let her go...

Finn launched off the bed, stumbled to the bathroom and with a quick flick of his wrist at the controls turned the shower spray to fast, hard and mind-numbingly cold.

There he stood, hands braced on the sandstone tiles, head bowed, while the water pounded his scalp and shoulders and he commanded his heart to stop beating for her. He shoved common sense down his throat until he nigh on choked on it, oblivious to time or place... Until bright light slashed through the room and a sharp, pained cry rent the air—

'Oh, my God, Finn! Your back. Baby, your back.'

Slam went his heart against the wall of his chest and he cursed inwardly. How could he have forgotten even for a moment? *Idiot.* This was what she did to him—banished thought until he operated like a loose cannon. Out of control. He hadn't wanted her seeing him like this, finding out this way.

Drenching his lungs with fortifying air, he commanded his heart to calm and relished the sanity that rained over him, bringing with it relief. So much relief it punctured his nape and made his head tip back until he stared at the white-wash on the ceiling.

It was over.

Now she'd loathe him. Just as he deserved. Hate him. Run. Far, far away from him. Before he hurt her, ruined her life beyond repair.

Slowly, inexorably, he allowed the cold to bleed into his veins, into his soul, until he was frozen to his emotional core. Braced for the highway to hell.

CHAPTER THIRTEEN

SCARS. SCARS ALL over his back. And she was shaking from head to foot, going all female crazy on him, her heart a searing fireball, acidic tears splashing the backs of her eyes—which was the wake-up call she needed to give herself a good shake. Careening into an emotional abyss wouldn't help anyone here, least of all him. But—*oh, God*—she could virtually feel his pain, as if the sensations of brutality had been exhumed from the Stygian depths of her memories. And her heart ached. *Ached* for him.

Serena snatched a thick warm towel from the rail, shut the water off and stepped behind the curved glass screen, striving to avert her gaze and failing miserably.

'You've been beaten,' she breathed, her throat clotted with anger and grief, because although time had endeavoured to heal him he'd been whipped and burned and— *Oh, my God...* 'When, Finn? When? How? Why?'

How could she not have known? Why hadn't he told her?

His torso swelled on a deep inhalation before his shoulders hardened to steel and he turned with excruciating slowness. Dark blond hair plastered his brow, falling into glacier-blue eyes as cold as the frigid droplets that clung to his naked skin.

A shiver shook her spine. Never had she seen him cold. Wouldn't have thought it possible from the man who beguiled the masses with his stunning smile and charismatic charm. It was the equivalent of dunking her in the Arctic.

'Singapore.'

One word, delivered in a voice so cool and sharp she knew it was just the tip of an iceberg.

'S...Singapore?' The floor tilted and her arm shot out to brace her weight; her palm slipped on a cool trickle of condensation as her brain was flooded with implications.

'Yes,' he said, devoid of emotion as he snagged the towel from her hand and wrapped it around his lean hips.

Singapore.

'Tell me...this has nothing to do with Tom,' she said, her voice barely audible as her mind whirled faster than the room. 'Tell me there's no connection. Because that would mean—'

Oh, no. Please, no.

'I've lied to you all along,' he admitted. Detached. Hateful.

Serena closed her eyes. 'I...I trusted you.'

She waited for the hot, pungent wash of anger and anguish to weave hotly through her veins, but all she kept envisaging were those barbaric scars marring his golden skin and all she felt was numb.

'No, you didn't, Serena. And if you were starting to it was against your better judgement, I'm sure.'

He was right, of course. She hadn't trusted him at all in the beginning. Amazing what the onslaught of sexual attraction could achieve. Gradually blinding her until a thick, dense veil of molten desire shrouded her eyes to what she'd suspected all along.

The truth she'd been waiting for all these months.

The truth this man had told her didn't exist.

Damn him. And damn her cursed heart too. How could she have been so naïve?

'I want the truth, Finn. And don't you dare lie to me again.'

'Put something on,' he ordered.

That chilly tone simultaneously made her shiver and feel bemused. Why was he being this way? So closed off. Aloof. Poles apart from the adoring, affectionate man she'd given her body to—as if he simply didn't care any more. The snaking suspicion that he never truly had coiled in her chest, constricting her lungs until her breath hissed past her throat.

No, wait. She would not think the worst of him again—not until she'd heard him out. There could be a perfectly good explanation for all this. Right? *Oh, God.*

'Here.'

He unhooked a white robe from the back of the door and she shoved her arms into the soft cotton, then tied the sash and nipped the lapels at her throat.

With an austere jerk of his head he motioned her towards the lounge area, where two cushy emerald-green armchairs sat at angles on either side of the marble fireplace. 'Have a seat. I just need a minute to dress.'

'I'd rather stand,' she said, altogether too jittery, needing the succulent warmth of the honey-coloured carpet brushing the soles of her feet to ground her somehow.

Every second was an endless stretch as her brain worked overtime. Then he reappeared, wearing a black T-shirt, low-slung jeans and a hardened façade that made her stomach tighten in response.

Just who *was* this man?

No daredevil swagger this night.

Gait stiff, body taut, he braced his forearm on the marble mantel and stared into the lifeless grate.

'We were taken from a private club in Singapore after our drinks were drugged. Out cold for about twelve hours. We woke up in an old wartime holding cell near the port.'

'You were…' *Breathe, Serena, breathe.* 'Taken? Like, for ransom?'

'Thirty million was the starting bid.'

Down she went, collapsing onto the nearest chair, while her thoughts tripped over one another. But when his meaning hit and collided with the imagery of his horrific scars the juxtaposition struck like a bolt of lightning and she began to shake. All over.

'Was…was Tom beaten like that?'

The hand at his hip balled into a tight fist and his legs flexed as he forced himself into the ground. For a split second she allowed herself the fantasy that he wanted to come to her, hold her.

'No,' he said, as black and hard as the mound of coal he was fixated on. 'He didn't suffer in that way.' Glancing up, he met her eyes, and for the first time she saw a frisson of emotion warm those ice-blue depths—sincerity. 'That's the absolute truth. So don't even picture it in your head. Didn't happen. Promise me you will remember that.'

She frowned, unsure what to believe. 'I don't understand. How come he wasn't touched when you were? It doesn't make sense.'

He held still, willing her to trust him—at least in this. It was important to him, she realised.

'Let's just say they had far more interest in me.'

What? Even that failed to compute. Why would criminals be partial to Finn—?

Air hit the back of her throat, where a great lump began to swell, and she bit down on her lips.

Panic flitted across his face. 'Hey, Serena, are you listening to me? Did you hear what I said?'

She swallowed thickly. 'You *made* them more interested in you.' He had an astonishing flair for it after all. 'You took the brunt of it, didn't you?' she asked, a little bit shocked, a whole lot awed.

Yet he merely hitched one shoulder in blatant insouciance as if it were nothing. *Nothing?* What? Did he think he'd deserved it, or something?

Switzerland… Sick…

'You were beaten so brutally that you spent months recovering in Switzerland, didn't you?' *In hiding.* 'And that is why you didn't come to Tom's funeral.' While she'd cursed and berated him, blind to it all.

'Yes,' he admitted.

Curse her throbbing heart, because the thought of him being alone, broken and torn, all that time in such pain...

His cerulean-blue eyes darkened dangerously as they narrowed on her face. 'Do not look at me with pity, Serena. I took your brother into that club. A club I knew was notorious. He *trusted* me.' Anger spewed from him, driven by the self-loathing that contorted his face. 'I led him into that hellhole and don't you forget it!'

Slapped with his fury, she rocked where she sat. Then she prompted her lungs to function properly as she sieved and scrutinised his way of thinking, only to recall their conversation on a harbour many moons ago.

'You didn't lead him, Finn. It was his choice. *His* choice. Back at Monaco you told me I wasn't responsible for the decisions he made. That I shouldn't feel guilt because he wouldn't want that. Are you going to tell me you lied about that too?'

Please don't. Because I'm already confused, wondering what has been real, and I'm afraid that every word from your mouth has been a lie.

'No, but—' His brow crunched for a beat. 'This is different.' Pushing off the mantel, he swung away and began to pace. 'I came out alive. He didn't.'

Now, *that* was a fact she couldn't dispute. To think that all this time she'd never known, had been kept in the dark—

'My God, Finn, did he even drown at all? What happened to him?'

Flinging himself down onto the opposite chair, he let the clasped ball of his white-knuckled hands dangle in the space between his open legs and met her gaze.

'Long story short: it was a get-rich-quick scheme run by some highly intelligent brains who had a perverted opinion of hospitality.'

He grimaced, as if the memories tasted vile on his tongue, and her heart thrashed for him.

'After about four days the bartering began, and on the fifth day they brought Tom in. Threatened him. Gave me the choice to do him over or they would.' A mirthless huff burst past his lips. 'The kid always looked at me like I was some kind of hero and there I was, inclined to knock him unconscious rather than allow the guards to maul him.'

The space behind her ribs inflated with his pain and her stomach gave a sickening twist. Because it was sick. Twisted. Perverted. 'Oh, Finn.' What a decision to have to make. It must have been torture for him—for them both.

'They knew fine and well he was my weakness, and I couldn't stand the lack of control.' With a rueful shake of his head he glanced towards the wide double doors leading to the balcony, where the strokes of dawn painted the sky in amber and gold. As if he searched for peace and beauty in the midst of such horror. 'To wrench some of it back I threw more money in the pot, and within two hours sixty million had been transferred from my Swiss bank account into one on the Cayman Islands.'

Self-derision twisted his full lips and her back crushed the downy cushions as she braced herself.

'It was a long shot, so I wasn't particularly surprised when two days later we were moved to an abandoned liner off the coast. I knew then we weren't getting out of there alive.' He jabbed his fingers through his hair. 'Tom was getting weak, losing his will. I got desperate. Bribed one of the guards to get him out. He could only take one of us for risk of getting caught. I didn't bother telling Tom. Didn't want him objecting to leaving me behind. He was an honourable kid.'

His voice cracked and the fissure streaked through her heart.

'Courageous too. You'd have been proud of him, Serena.'

Her trembling fingers slapped over her mouth to capture the sob that gathered force in her chest and burned the base of her throat. After all they'd been through together she was *not* going to break in front of Finn. She was not going to be weak.

'Next night, as planned, the guard smuggled him out. Whether he was anxious to get back before his absence was noticed or whether there was a struggle, I don't know, but he decided to drop him close to the port...'

His devastating gaze locked on hers, filled with pain, such heart-wrenching pain, that she sank her blunt nails into her palms, trying to stay motionless...

'So he could swim the half-mile to the shore.'

'Oh, no,' she breathed.

'Serena, I didn't know—or I would've warned the guard. I didn't know he could barely swim and I sent him to his death.'

The walls of her chest clamped vice-like as she shook with the effort not to crack. She had to stay strong for both of them. It was all so tragic. So heartbreakingly unfair.

Swallowing thickly, she prayed her voice wouldn't rupture. 'You couldn't have known unless he'd told you. He was really embarrassed about it.'

He'd been petrified of deep water too, but there was no way she was telling Finn that; he had enough to carry on his conscience. *Oh, Tom, I'm so sorry I wasn't there for you.*

Back she went, hurtling towards the emotional precipice, her eyes pooling with moisture. God, how did she make them stop? Averting her face, she blinked rapidly as her defences began to splinter.

Apparently she wasn't the only one, because in a flash Finn was striding across the floor and plunging to his knees in front of her. *Her* Finn.

Moving in between her legs, he brushed a lock of hair from her temple in a tender graze and pressed his lips to her cheek. 'I'm sorry. I'm sorry. So sorry I took him from you.'

The sound of his voice, so broken and desolate, slapped some strength into her spine and she cupped his face with a firm, warm touch and hardened her voice.

'You didn't take him from me. *They* took him from me. It was not your fault.'

'How can you say that? I am the sole reason he is gone. They wanted my money, Serena.'

'No. If that were true they would have taken just you. They saw an opportunity and they took it. Don't you see? You were both in the wrong place at the wrong time.'

His jaw tight enough to crack a filling, he frowned deeply. 'I sent him out there.'

'You were trying to save his life. It was a tragedy borne from their actions, not yours.'

A sense of *déjà vu* flirted with her mind. How many times had someone said that to *her* after the attack? Yet had she ever truly believed them? No. Since Finn had come into her world she'd realised her life was built on shaky foundations and she'd never truly moved on.

She didn't want that for him. To be trapped in some kind of stasis, haunted by the past.

She swept his damp hair back from his brow and his eyelids grew heavy. 'This is going to ruin you, Finn. This guilt that is driving you. I want it to stop. Tom wouldn't want this.'

Finn's frustration ignited and he jerked from her grasp, bolted to his feet and veered away from her. 'That's your emotions talking after sharing a bed with a born seducer. Sooner or later it will pass and you'll blame me—hate me as you should.'

'I'll never hate you, Finn. Ever. Nor will I blame you. You need to accept that.'

For an infinitesimal moment he simply stared at her. His expression was pinched with pain, but it was the intense flare in his cerulean eyes that lifted her spirits. Hope was reflected there…faith that slowly diminished as if the lights were going out in his soul.

'Serena, don't you see what you're doing? You're allowing good sex to drive your emotions and cloud your judgement. Already you've forgotten that I've lied to you for months.'

Unwilling even to consider how easily incredible sex could be downgraded to 'good' within hours—she wasn't ready for that reality just yet—she felt a burst of unease fire through her stomach. Nothing had been forgotten. But some sixth sense beat an ominous warning that his answers would never suffice. Only hurt. Badly.

Ignoring the tumultuous roil inside her, she lifted her chin. 'First off, don't speak to me like I'm some female and I don't know my own mind. I promise you it's not misted by desire up there. But maybe now is a good time to tell me why. Why you lied to me. Why, almost a year later, I would still be in the dark if I hadn't walked in on you tonight.'

The more she considered it, the more bewildered she became. And, if she were honest, there was a good dose of humiliation in there at her naïvety too. Once again she'd fallen into the hands of deceit, and the fact that those hands belonged to Finn was a bitter pill to swallow.

Finn flung the double doors wide, inviting the bite of British morning air to swirl around her ankles. Then he braced his hands on the overhead frame and looked out onto the green acreage surrounding the Country Club, the golden wash of dawn warming his pale complexion.

'Fact is Tom's drowning ruffled the rogue guard and he tipped off the Singapore police to my whereabouts.'

It wasn't difficult to comprehend the acrid tinge to his dark voice—Tom's death had likely saved Finn from a worse fate and *that* was anathema to him.

'The brains behind the operation disappeared—the ransom too, through laundering. There have been a few leads but it's slow going. We didn't want you in any danger, getting caught up in the ongoing investigation. I suggested you were told the same story as everyone else. Your dad agreed. He didn't want you hurting any more than you already were.'

'Wow, tough love must have gone by the wayside that day.' Then again, Michael Scott couldn't handle her at the best of times. Showing his love didn't come naturally or easily.

'Plus,' he began warily, his arms plunging to his sides, 'I kind of promised Tom I would look out for you. Make sure you didn't go looking for blood.'

The rush of anger drained away as quickly as it had come, leaving a numb sensation bleeding into every inch of her. Yeah, that was exactly what Tom would have done. But that wasn't the reason she crossed her arms over her chest to calm the dark storm brewing behind her ribs.

'Would this promise to look out for me be the reason you offered to be my friend weeks ago?' *Say no. Say no.*

Keeping his gaze averted, he shoved his hands into deep denim pockets. 'You could say that, yes.'

Whack. His words punched her midriff, making her flinch. 'That's very...*noble* of you, Finn.' Was that really her voice? That cracked melody of sarcasm and bitterness? A portrayal of a heart betrayed.

There she'd been, blissfully ignorant, revelling in the idea that he wanted to spend time with her. God, she'd even lux-uriated in the way his guilt had eased, making him more content—had rejoiced in the sanguine expectation that *she* was the reason for it. And all the while he'd been keeping a promise. While she could grasp his need to, as far as she was concerned as soon as their friendship had developed into more they'd gone way beyond that. Why not just tell her be-fore they slept together? It felt like dishonesty.

'You know what really gets to me?' she said, pleading with her strength not to abandon her now. 'Every day you omitted to tell me the truth, and every night I came closer to...' *To falling for you.* 'To trusting you. To sharing your bed. How could you do that, Finn? Lie with me...' *Make love to me with such intensity.* 'While keeping something so huge, so important to me a secret?' *Give me a good reason, please.*

When he finally turned to face her, one corner of his

mouth lifted ruefully. 'I've never pretended to be a saint, Serena. The sinner in me simply couldn't resist you.'

Their eyes caught...held...and she told herself she was misreading the fierce fervour in his gaze. That all along she'd imagined the emotional pull. If he'd felt more for her he would have had the decency to tell her the truth well before he'd taken her body. *What had you been secretly hoping for, Serena? That he was falling like you were? You're a fool.*

'I warned you, baby. That you were making the biggest mistake of your life.'

Yes, he had. *'So be it,'* she'd said, and here she was.

The cyclone of torment in her chest picked up pace and the strain of keeping her head high wrought a deep throb in the muscle of her nape.

It was a foolish heart and a fledgling female pride that spoke. 'Tell me something, Finn. Is every woman your *baby* too?' *Please say no.* In truth, she wished the words right back. Didn't want to hear she'd meant nothing to him. A silly, stupid girly part of her wanted to keep hoping she'd been different from all the others. Special in some way. As unique as he'd frequently told her.

A muscle ticked in his jaw and his brow pinched for one, two, three beats of her thundering heart. Then he hitched one broad shoulder in insouciance.

'Naturally.'

And just like that her stomach hollowed and she felt emptier than she ever had before.

'Naturally,' she repeated, with all the blasé indifference she could muster as she fought the anguished throb of her body.

Lashes weighted, she allowed them to fall until he disappeared.

Serena Scott—one of many. Like all the nameless faces that had wandered through his life. Her father's too. A woman she'd sworn she'd never become.

Anger hit her like an explosion of fire. At him, yes, but

equally at herself. For opening up once again. Being susceptible, vulnerable to a man.

Why did unlocking your heart, daring to dream, have to hurt so much? Have to end in crushing heartbreak and pain? There she'd been, lying blissfully in his arms, believing every word from his lips. Sure he was coming to feel more for her, that she was enough to hold his attention. Teasing her mind's eye with more blissful nights, more exciting wonderful days. A future.

Enough.

On a long sigh she opened her eyes. Literally and figuratively.

Thank God she'd discovered the truth before she'd fallen in love with him. It was petrifying to think how close she'd come to doing just that.

'Serena?'

That deep voice, now perturbed, laced with concern, brought her attention back to where he stood.

Ah. Worried he'd hurt her, was he? Well, admittedly she'd love to rail and scream at him, but the little pride she had left was too precious. When she walked out of this suite it would be with her head high and dignity roiling inside her.

In fairness, he'd never pretended to be honourable with regards to women, and he'd warned her over and over. It was hardly his fault she'd strived to be a player, convinced she knew the rules, adamant that she'd come out unscathed. Instead she'd believed every expertly practised word. Misread every artful amorous touch.

How could she have been so naïve? Again! Lesson learned.

Moreover, right now the man teetered on the edge of a black abyss and she refused to be the one to push him over—she'd vacationed in hell before, and the view wasn't pretty.

Fear. Flashbacks. Nightmares. Menace surrounding you, burrowing into your soul. It didn't take a genius to figure out his erratic behaviour on and off the track in the last few months now either. Even his own survival was anathema to him. He wished he'd died too. Or more likely instead of Tom.

Come to think of it—dread curdled with her pique, making her stomach churn violently—it was entirely plausible that he was suffering from some kind of survivor's guilt. She'd read about that somewhere—probably a pamphlet in some clinic. And if that were true he needed help.

Somewhat reluctant to bathe in those beautiful eyes, she met them regardless. 'Forget about you and me. We both knew it was just sex and now it's over.' His throat convulsed but she was determined not to read anything into it. Bad enough that she'd imagined he flinched. 'I'll never be ashes in your wake, Finn. You know me better than that.'

'Good. That's good.' Relief soothed his taut features and he padded out onto the balcony and gripped the iron railing—white knuckles stark over black.

Why could she still feel his pain as if it was a living, breathing entity inside her, melding with her own? As if they were bonded somehow? Heavens, it *hurt*.

Serena glanced at the door leading to her suite and escape beckoned like an old friend. Her feet itched to run until she was too exhausted to feel anything. 'I should go,' she said abruptly. 'We both need some sleep.' If she felt battered and bruised from riding an emotional roller coaster he had to feel just as bad.

Which was likely why she couldn't move. Found herself ensnared in a vicious primal pull. Honestly, it was like turning her back on a wounded animal. She couldn't do it. Despite everything, she couldn't leave without trying one last time.

The problem was no matter what she said no words were going to convince him he wasn't to blame.

Frustration ate at her.

Leaving her angry aching heart indoors, she followed him onto the balcony. A crazy notion stirred up a hornets' nest inside her even as she winced at the risk, at how he'd react, and wondered if she could even manage it without shattering.

Easy, she came up behind him. 'Don't get a fright,' she said softly, echoing his sentiment from the cabaret at Montreal. A night from her dreams… With deft speed she slammed the door on her reminiscing. *Focus.*

His honed frame tensed.

'Finn, it's okay.' She laid her hands on his back, as gentle and calming as if he were a skittish colt. She smoothed them around his waist, wrapped her arms about him and pressed her cheek to the soft, freshly laundered fabric of his T-shirt.

'Serena,' he choked out, muscles flexing as his grip tightened on the rail.

After a *'Shh…'* that ripped her soul, his shoulders dropped and he began to ease.

'Let me?' she asked, tiptoeing her fingers beneath the hem of his T and tentatively inching the material upwards before she pulled back.

One look at the deep white criss-cross lines that marred the centre of his back, the puckered skin between his shoulder blades, and her chest ached viciously. Tears pooled, brimmed once more, and this time she let them fall. Unable to stop the rain. Surely she owed Tom nothing less.

Boys don't cry, Serena.

Well, this *girl* did.

Silent tears seared her swollen throat—for him, for Tom—as she leaned forward and tenderly kissed his back once, twice, before she rubbed her cheek against him gingerly, affectionately.

'Thank you,' she whispered, her voice as raw as her heart. 'Thank you for making his last days bearable. For protecting him for me. For trying to save his life.'

'Serena…' he breathed, almost longingly, as his big body trembled.

'Please don't let his death be for nothing. You have your entire life ahead of you. He'd want you to live it.'

Torso convulsing, he hung his head.

Enough. No more. It was all over now.

Serena let the fabric fall and trailed her fingers down his sides in goodbye. Then she turned and walked away with her head held high. Ready to fight another day.

CHAPTER FOURTEEN

THE SILVERSTONE CIRCUIT was an almighty roar and the chant of Finn's name from his fiercest homeland supporters rang in his ears as he stepped off the winner's podium with a farewell wave and shot through the crowd. He hadn't seen Serena since dawn, and the perpetual torment from his heart and conscience had him hurtling towards insanity.

He had to see her. Check she was okay. In truth he'd swear he could feel her pain, and his arms ached to hold her—hell, his entire body ached for her. Had done since the moment she'd vanished from his suite. Since she'd ripped his heart out by pleading with him to live his life. The way she'd touched him so affectionately, forgivingly, would stay with him always.

It had taken every ounce of strength he possessed to keep his hands fisted on the iron rail, not to turn around and reach for her. But no matter how hard he tried he couldn't believe for one second that she could forgive him. He was convinced the only reason she hadn't looked at him with hate in her eyes was because of the incredible night they'd shared. Or maybe he'd taken Tom's place in her world. A rebounding kind of need.

Eventually, when she realised that, she'd walk away—and he'd be in so deep it would kill him. He'd lose her. Just as he lost everyone he cared for. It was inevitable.

So, while it had torn him apart to sever their connection, he knew it was for the best. For both of them.

In and out of the Scott Lansing garage he went—his guts twisting at the barren space—before he jogged round to the back of the pits, where a myriad of luxurious motor homes were parked.

Smooth tarmac gave way to the crunch of gravel beneath his boots and dark shadows crawled eerily over the dirt, up over the high-gloss black paintwork of the fleet, as if thick, ominous clouds slowly usurped the sun. He shuddered...

Then crashed to a halt.

There stood Michael Scott, at the bottom of the steps to Finn's motor home, wearing an expression that weakened his knees.

Skin clammy, he clutched at his chest, felt the thrash of his heart against his palm. 'Wha...what's happened?' *No, please God no. Please let her be okay.*

'What you've got to understand about Serena, my boy, is that when her emotions get too big for her she runs. Always has, since she was a little girl.' Regret deepened his voice. 'Don't suppose it helped that she never had a mother in her life. I take it you told her everything?'

Finn tried to swallow as relief and heartache vied for space behind his ribs. She'd left him. 'Yes. Everything.' Then he remembered the phone call he'd taken before the race. 'The police in Singapore have just made an arrest.'

The older man took one step forward and laid a heavy hand on Finn's shoulder. 'Good. Now we'll get some justice. I know you tried to do right by my son.'

Finn locked on to Mick's sincere gaze, desperate to believe him.

'Serena must know it too, considering all your body parts are intact. Time to move on, Finn. Let it go.'

Maybe he nodded; he was too numb to be sure.

'Can't guarantee she'll come back in a hurry. Last time,

after the funeral, she was away months. She's not going to London. I know that much. But she did leave you this.'

Michael passed him a white envelope, with Finn's name a messy scrawl across the front, then patted his shoulder and sidestepped to walk past.

'By the way, she watched the race—asked me to say you were awesome out there and that you'll know what she means.'

A ghost of a smile touched his lips. Finally the woman uttered the words he'd tried to tease out of her for months. *Aw, man*, was it any wonder he adored her?

'Yeah, I do. Thanks, Mick.'

Bones weighted with dread, he plonked down on the top rung of his steps and thumbed the sticky flap of the envelope. Patience wasn't his strong suit and after two seconds he tore it apart, until her letter was in his hands.

On a long exhale he unfolded the crisp sheet and stared for a long moment, watching a fine drizzle dust the page.

Despite the chaotic churning of emotions inside him, her messy handwriting brought another smile to his lips. He missed her already.

Dear Finn,

I've never been one for goodbyes, but in the last few weeks you've helped me say another kind of goodbye—to Tom, so I could lay him to rest. Despite how our friendship came about you've been a friend to me in many ways, shown me much about my life, and I'd like to return the favour. So I'm calling in the wish you owe me.

Now, I know what you're thinking: my logic is a bit backward—how can my favour be your wish? But hear me out, okay?

It dawned on me earlier, when I left, that it doesn't matter if you never believe my word or believe in my forgiveness. What truly matters is that you learn to forgive yourself. Otherwise, and trust me when I say this, you'll never truly move on. Which is why I'm about to tell you something very few people know and I'm asking you to keep it close to your chest.

Long story short, as you would say, my first naïve crush was with one of Tom's friends. One who quickly turned hostile. And for a long time I blamed myself for what happened afterwards.

I should probably explain that I was young, with no women around, and not really sure how to handle boys. I figured I'd rather be one of them, and that was fine until I came to that awkward age where they began to treat me differently. Anyway, I was fourteen, and let's just say I liked this much older boy—or should I say man? He was Tom's age: nineteen.

He weaved his web, spun his lies, told me anything and everything—'I want you, Serena, I love you. Come meet me, Serena, I won't hurt you'—until I fell for him. I started to dress up—girly stuff—flirted a little, sneaked out with him, but I wasn't prepared for what came back at me.

Turns out 'no' didn't mean no with him.

The first time he tried to force me I managed to get away, and he persuaded me not to tell Tom or he would hurt him. Foolish, I know, but I think it's easy to believe anything at that age. Spider-Man comes to mind...

Anyway, he began to follow me, watch me from the shadows, and I was frightened for a long time. Then one night, during a huge party downstairs, he came up to my bedroom. He'd been drinking. He overpowered me. I was beaten up pretty bad, among other things, and I'm sure he would've gone all the way if Tom hadn't come in.

There was a huge fight and Tom got seriously

hurt—we thought he'd never drive again—but he pulled through. Of course he blamed himself for not reading the signs sooner, so you see I'm not surprised he asked you to watch out for me. He became very protective.

I saw a counsellor for many months and she tried to help me past it. In many ways she did. She made me accept that I didn't ask for it. I didn't deserve to be beaten. She certainly helped me to stand tall, but in reality I never truly moved on. I didn't completely let go of the blame. Of the thought that if I'd been braver, stronger, told someone sooner, Tom's health and career wouldn't have hung in the balance for so long.

I didn't let go of the idea that my behaviour was at fault. Because if I had I wouldn't have suppressed the woman I am inside.

You've shown me that, Finn. Helped me see so many things. But watching you struggle this morning I realised I'm still searching for peace.

Choices.

I'm choosing to let go, Finn. To forgive myself. I wish you would too.

At the bottom of this note is the number of the counsellor I saw, and my wish is that you go and see her, even if it's just the once. She can help you if you'll let her. It's strange, but I used to resent my dad for sending me—just thought he was palming me off on someone else. But I can see now. He was too close to the situation. Too emotionally involved. Which is why I think you need to speak to someone who isn't personally connected, you know?

You're a survivor. We both are. Let's make the most of this life we have. If not for us, for Tom.

Well, that's it, I guess. Take care of yourself and try not to crash my car, okay? Look after her. She

*may be a fiery bolt of lightning with a tough outer
shell but underneath...she's still just a girl.
Serena.*

The paper fluttered to the dirt as Finn leaned his elbows
on his knees and pressed the heels of his hands to his eyes.
Moisture smothered his palms as his shoulders shook in the
suffocating silence.

Underneath...she's still just a girl.

Idiot. He was such an idiot. He hadn't just hurt her; he'd
caused more damage than he'd ever dreamed possible.

Was it any wonder she'd stifled her femininity? And what
had he done? Given her confidence, told her she was unique
in every way, encouraged her to open up to him. And in the
next breath, fuelled by his own fears, he'd insinuated that
she was just another good-time girl who meant nothing to
him, expecting her to take it like the tough cookie she was—
and succeeded in stripping her raw. Forgetting for one moment that *underneath she's still just a girl*. One who'd been
tampered with when she'd been merely fourteen years old.

Against all the odds, no matter what life threw at her, she
came out fighting.

'You have no idea how proud I am of you,' he murmured,
to no one but himself, wishing she was here and he could
hold her. 'How brave and beautiful and strong and amazing you are to me.'

Finn rubbed his eyes, then clawed down his face.

Why did he keep hurting people? He knew not to let his
emotions engage. Knew he was like a loose cannon, made
bad choices. He'd left Eva to suffer, sent Tom to his death.
Now he'd hurt Serena too.

What was more she'd been betrayed barely out of adolescence and now Finn had done it a second time. She'd never
trust him again—not in a million years.

Any last vestige of hope died in his soul as she disappeared with his heart.

He needed more than some shrink. He needed a miracle. One perfectly beautiful little miracle.

Every cell in his body screamed for him to go and find her, make it all better somehow. But what would he say? *I'm sorry* didn't sound anywhere near what she deserved. And that was all he had to offer. Apart from more hurt in the long run. He was messed up and he knew it. He also knew he was far better off alone.

He just had to hope she found the peace and happiness she deserved.

As for him, he had a wish to take care of.

He owed his girl nothing less.

CHAPTER FIFTEEN

Five weeks and two days later...

THE MONZA POST-RACE party was the epitome of Italian style and elegance, held in the vast courtyard of a lavish hotel. But the midnight sky, twinkling with diamanté brilliance, acted as the perfect ceiling and only served to remind Serena of a magnificent tent in Montreal.

Champagne spurted from a towering ice sculpture like an ivory waterfall, to pool and froth at the base. But the bubbly effervescence only struck a chord of the Silverstone Ball.

Closing her eyes momentarily, she breathed in the sweet calming scent of the wisteria draping the balconies overhead and turned to her dad. 'I have no idea how you talked me into this. I've only been back a few hours. I could be in my PJs, eating nachos and watching a movie right now.'

Instead she was a nausea-inducing swarm of anticipation in killer heels, trying to perfect a smile that said she was having a ball. All the while wondering if he would come, who he would bring, what she would say to him. So much for the blasé *oh-hi-how-are-you?* she'd been hoping for at tomorrow's meeting.

'Yes, well, frankly I was getting sick and tired of the "I *vhant* to be alone" Greta Garbo routine. I'll only let you hide for so long, Serena.'

'I wasn't trying to hide,' she hissed.

'Whatever you say, sweetheart.'

Serena sighed. She'd just wanted their first hello to be on equal ground, and she refused to think less of herself for that. Not after she'd spent weeks trying to get over the man she'd purged her soul for. Writing that letter had taken her back, splintered her defences, but the thought of him hurting, being in so much pain, had somehow outweighed her survival instincts. And if the tabloids were to be believed he was back on top form, oozing charisma with that legendary smile of his, so it was worth it to see him happy. Moving on.

True, seeing him with another woman had been...hard, but she'd needed that push to move on. Now she was just... peachy.

Which didn't really explain why the sight of her dad smiling devilishly at some curvy blonde sparked her off. 'I don't get this "variety is the spice of life" business. What exactly is so wonderful about variety when they all look the same? There's something cold about it. About them.'

She couldn't understand the appeal. Not compared to the hours of scorching bliss she'd experienced in Finn's arms— all the more intense for the way she'd felt, she was sure.

'That's the point. It doesn't mean anything. It's safe.'

'That's like going on a ghost train with your eyes shut. Going through the motions—'

'With none of the emotions. Exactly. For me, it's because I'll always love your mother. She was The One for me. All the others since were just flash and no substance. Safe. A way to ease the loneliness, I guess.'

Serena frowned up at him as the floor did a funny little tilt. When she'd been a little girl she'd often asked about her mum. He'd tried to talk about her, but as she'd got older she'd thought his struggle and avoidance meant he hadn't truly loved her. But clearly he'd loved her intensely.

A pang of bittersweet happiness eased the ache in her chest. To think it had been *her mother* who'd had the power to win his heart. It explained so much about him. She almost asked him for more, but this wasn't the time or the place. Instead she murmured, 'Never thought of it that way.'

Safe. Untouched. That suited Finn to perfection too, didn't it? The showman who wore his charming façade to veil the tortured man beneath. But, unlike her mum, Serena hadn't been enough to win his heart.

'Don't suppose you're thinking about Finn right now?'

'I'm doing nothing of the sort,' she said, casting him a dour look before she did something stupid like burst into tears. When she was supposed to be peachy!

His graphite eyes twinkled knowingly before his handsome face took on a contemplative look etched with remorse.

'I doubt I've given you much decent advice in your life. I was ill-equipped to deal with two young kids—especially you. That's something I'll always be sorry for, Serena. But when I lost her I had to...'

Her voice as raw as her throat, Serena quietly finished for him. 'Get up. Get busy. Move on.' For all their sakes.

He gave her a rueful smile. 'But let me tell you this. If you're anything like me, or all the Scotts before you, you'll get one shot at true happiness. If you think Finn's The One don't let him go without a fight.'

Serena bit her bottom lip to stop it trembling. 'I'm not interested.' It didn't matter how much she hurt, how much she wanted, she was never opening up again. 'Anyway, he's already moved on.'

'You sure about that? Because the man who came to see me yesterday, asking for some time off so he could go gallivanting to find...' he made inverted comma actions with his fingers '..."his girl" didn't look like he'd moved on to me.'

A paralysing ball of hope bounced in her chest and she swiftly batted it away. No more foolish daydreaming. 'He has "girls" on every continent. He's moved on, I'm telling you.'

'Positive? Because that same guy, who's just walked through the archway, clapped eyes on you and looks like he's been hit with a semi-truck, is on his way over.'

'Oh, my life.' She wasn't ready—nowhere near ready.

'So you might want to get rid of that deer-in-the-headlights look and bear in mind another of Garbo's sayings.'

Huh? 'Which is?'

'Anyone who has a continuous smile on his face conceals a toughness that is almost frightening.'

'And why should that affect me?'

'No smile tonight. I get the feeling the shackles are off. I hope you're ready for this sweetheart.'

Right now the only thing she was ready for was to launch herself over the twelve-foot stone wall encircling the courtyard. She would have done if she hadn't been wandering around Europe aimlessly for the last month, only to find herself in some café in Paris, nursing a lacklustre cappuccino and the realisation that it didn't matter how far she ran, her aching heart still lay inside her chest and the memories lingered. Peace was nowhere to be found and solitude just made the emptiness deeper. She had to face him. Prove to herself she was over him.

'How far?' Appalled by her serious case of the jitters, she nailed her feet to the paved slabs. *'How far?'*

An unholy glee lit up her father's graphite eyes. 'Thirty feet and closing.'

She stifled the urge to smooth her riotous mane, insanely grateful that she'd developed a fetish for dresses, and silently chanted an endless loop of, *He will not affect me. I am completely over him. He will not affect—*

'Good evening, Miss Seraphina Scott.'

Ohh, this was not good. 'This' being the hellish swarm of fireflies lighting up her midriff in a mad, wild rush at the mere sound of his rich, sinful drawl.

More than a little woozy, she focused on turning gracefully, determined not to fall at his feet. She took a deep breath, raised her chin, then pivoted on her entirely too adventurous heels…

And went up in flames.

Doomed. She was totally and utterly doomed.

Dressed in a sharp black custom-fit suit and a thin silk tie, as if he'd just stepped off a movie set, Finn St George struck a stunning pose of insolent flair. All potent masculinity and devilish panache.

Confident as ever. A little arrogant. A whole lot bold.

Pure joy lapped at her senses—she'd missed him so much.

All that deliberately unkempt dirty blond hair was now long enough to curl over the collar of his crisp white shirt and that face... *Oh, my life*, he was so amazingly beautiful.

No depraved gleam in those cerulean blues tonight. Fantastical as the idea was, she fancied those eyes were darkly intense, savagely focused on her—a hunter stalking the ultimate prey. After weeks of living a dull, aching existence her body came alive, as if it recognised its mate, and her heart fluttered, trying to break free from the confines of her chest—

Serena slammed the cage shut and stamped on the brakes of her speeding thoughts. She would *not* misread those practised looks or his artful words. Not ever again.

He made her vulnerable to him with a click of his übertalented fingers, but demons would dance with angels before he stole more of her heart or her pride. So she dug out the biggest smile in *her* arsenal and directed her voice to super-sweet.

'Hey, Lothario, miss me?'

He wanted her now. *Now!* Fiercely. Possessively. Permanently.

When Mick Scott had texted him twenty minutes ago— *Guess whose girl is here?*—Finn hadn't trusted his luck but had tossed some clothes on nonetheless.

Now if he could just get over the shattering bodily impact of his first sight of her in weeks maybe he could think straight. As it was he had claws digging into his guts, demanding he haul her into his arms, delve into those fiery locks and slash his mouth over hers. But he reckoned since he'd messed up so catastrophically that winning her heart was going to require some finesse.

Mick eased by, patted Finn's shoulder and murmured, 'Try not to mess it up this time.'

Finn swallowed. Hard. Then told himself to forget about his boss and focus on his future. His entire life wrapped in a sensational electric-blue sheath. If she'd have him. Forgive him. Let him love her. Because that was all he had—his love.

This was it. The greatest risk of all. Because nothing came close to the potent charge of adrenaline that barrelled through his system when he was within ten feet of her. Fifty championships wouldn't even come close.

Had he missed her?

'I certainly have, Miss Scott. In fact I can easily say I've been miserable since the moment you left.'

He'd been plunged back into another hellhole, this one definitely of his own making, and he was determined to rectify that, no matter how long it took.

Granted, his admission hadn't worked the way he'd hoped—not if the stunned flash of incredulity in her sparkling grey gaze was anything to go by. Even the two feet separating them was a hot whirlpool that snap, crackled and popped with her pique.

Aw, man, maybe he was playing this all wrong. But the truth was he was nervous. *Him.* The man who flirted with death and had practically invented the word *reckless*.

'Yeah, okay, which is why you've already moved on and couldn't even spare me a phone call.'

Finn shoved his hands into his trouser pockets in case he lost his tenuous grip and just kissed the living daylights out of her. 'I wanted to give you some time to figure out how you feel. It hasn't been easy for me, Serena. It's been bloody agonising. You have no idea how many times I drove to the airport—'

'Going on holiday, were you?'

If his guts weren't writhing in a chaotic mess he would smile. That sassy mouth drove him crazy. Always had. And clearly she'd re-erected those barriers of hers. Well, he'd just have to pull them down all over again. He was fighting to win, and Finn St George always won.

'Dance with me?' He held out his hand. 'Give me your first dance—the one we didn't share back at Silverstone. Please?'

The truth was he just wanted to hold her. If he could make her remember what they were like together maybe she'd give him a chance.

She took so long to make her decision—her flawless brow nipped as she scrutinised his face—that Finn was headed for an aneurysm by the time her dubious voice, said, 'Okay. One dance.'

Before she changed her mind he grabbed her hand and practically dragged her across the courtyard—weaving around tables to a space right at the back of the dance floor, dimly lit, semi-private and leading to the gardens beyond.

Then he wrapped his hands around her dainty waist and hauled her into the tight circle of his arms to sway to an Italian love ballad. *Perfect.* She felt amazing, and when her deliciously evocative scent wrapped around his senses the ice in his veins started to melt.

'Finn,' she squeaked. 'I can hardly breathe.'

'Breathing is highly overrated. Do you really need to?' This was bliss for him and, selfish as it was, he was taking what he could while he could. *To hell with that. You're gonna win her back—she isn't leaving you again.*

'Yes, I do. I…'

She softened against him, twined her arms around his neck, and that glorious frisson of pleasure and pain jolted his heart.

When he pulled her closer still, crushing her soft breasts to his chest, a moan slipped past her lips—the kind she made when she was naked and sprawled all over him. Blood rushed to his head, making him simultaneously dizzy and hard. Not to mention astoundingly possessive—which he figured must be the reason he put his big fat foot in it.

'Have you been…seeing anyone?'

The spark of her ire crackled in the air and she stiffened in his arms.

Seriously? Could he be making a worse job of this? Where was his famed charm and charisma? Gone. Obliterated. By a five-foot-four spectacular bundle of fire.

'You've got some nerve,' she whispered furiously. 'Spouting rubbish about missing me, accusing me of seeing someone else, holding me as if you're petrified I'm going to vanish into thin air when you couldn't even last three weeks!'

Reluctantly he pulled back a touch. 'Three weeks before what?'

'Quenching your carnal appetites,' she hissed.

Finn just shook his head. 'You've lost me, beautiful.'

'Does Hungary ring any bells? Your much publicised photographs with some flashy starlet were all over the front page, so don't give me any bull crap.'

He couldn't help it. He grinned for the first time in aeons. 'You're jealous, baby.' *Aw, man,* he was definitely in with a chance. She had to feel something for him. *Had* to.

Her gorgeous face got madder still. 'I am not jealous at all. I don't give a flying fig who you dance the horizontal tango with—and don't you *dare* call me baby.'

Damn. What had possessed him to suggest she was one of many? A woman who'd witnessed her own father go through women like rice puffs.

'I never touched that actress, beautiful. It just so happens that was the only gig I went to and the woman couldn't take the hint so I left. There's been no one since you. In fact, you're the only woman I've slept with in well over a year.'

Those impossibly long sooty lashes fluttered over and over.

'Oh…'

And when she softened once more victory was a balmy rush, blooming out all over his skin.

Needing her taste in his mouth, he stole a lush, moist kiss from her lips. 'What's more I've never called anyone baby but you, Serena. And I never will. Because you're mine.' Another kiss. Then another. 'All mine. Unique in every single way—'

Suddenly she wrenched from his hold, took a step back.

'You've never called anyone baby but me, Finn? So you either lied to me then or you're lying now. Either way, I'm not interested. I...I can't do this again with you.'

The pain darkening her grey gaze punched him in the heart.

'I don't know if I can trust anything you say. I don't even know if your touch is real.'

The blood drained to his toes and a cold sweat chased it. 'You can. I'll prove it to you—

'Look, I just flew in a few hours ago and I could do with some sleep. I'll see you tomorrow, okay?'

Before he could say a word she darted off, swerving around the other couples on the dance floor.

Finn scrubbed a hand over his face. Okay. Maybe he should give her more time. The problem was, he couldn't abide her thinking she meant nothing to him. He was beginning to realise he'd made another huge mistake in not going after her sooner. But he'd been broken and he'd wanted to be whole. For her.

Oh, to hell with it.

Finn caught her up halfway to the exit, mid-throng.

'Oh, no you don't,' he said, swerving to block her path. She looked up, all flushed cheeks and wide eyes. Yet he couldn't decide if she was astonished that he'd chased her or that he was garnering them an audience.

'I'll follow you to the far ends of the earth, Serena.'

As for the onlookers—if he had to unveil the real Finn

St George to the world, show them the vulnerable man beneath to win her back, so be it.

'You're not getting away from me this time. I let you run once because I was scared, but I won't make the same mistake twice. I've made too many mistakes with you and I'll be damned if I make another.'

Finn would swear he could have heard a pin drop.

Until she breathed, 'Scared?'

'Terrified. But I'm not any more. I love you. You hear that, baby? I. Love. You.' Then, in front of hundreds of guests, he cupped her astounded face in his palms and kissed her with everything he was. With all the love in his heart and the need roiling inside him. Until neither of them could breathe and her shock gave way to desire. To the incredible bond he could feel pulling at his soul.

'Tell me you feel this,' he whispered over her lips.

'I...I feel this.'

'This has never been a lie, beautiful.'

Now came the hard part, he acknowledged. Convincing her that he meant every single word.

Dazed and disorientated, Serena suddenly found herself being lowered to her feet beneath a secluded pergola in gardens enchanted by moonlight. The wolf whistles and the roar of the crowd still rang in her ears and her lips were swollen from the wild crush of his ardour...

'Did you really just do that?' He'd kissed her in front of everyone. She was sure he had. Then he'd carried her out of there. He must have.

Sucking in air, she inhaled the minty scent of dew-drenched leaves as Finn took a step back, his eyes dark with desire, gleaming with intent.

Heat skittered through her veins. She felt hunted, and it was the most sensational, awesome, stupendous feeling in the world. If only her pesky inner voice would cease whispering doubt because she'd been seduced by his charm before.

'Finn? You do realise that come tomorrow morning the whole world will know you've just told me…' She still wasn't sure she'd heard him right. Or perhaps the truth of it was she couldn't bear to hope. To dream.

'That I love you? Good. It's about time. Then everyone will know that you're off limits.'

His voice was thick and possessive and dominating and it made her shiver. 'And you too!'

'That's the point, Serena.' Tenderly, he stroked his knuckles down her cheek. 'Because until you start believing that I'm yours and you're mine we're going nowhere. Until you believe that you're the only woman in the world for me there'll always be doubt. I've lost your trust, and I need to win it back before it's too late and I lose you forever.'

The impact of his words, his touch, his closeness, was earth-shattering. 'Just be honest with me, Finn. That's all I want.'

'And that's what you're going to get. Always.' His chest swelled as he inhaled deeply. 'I let you believe our friendship had been because of a promise I made to Tom, but that was just an excuse I gave myself to be with you. To spend time with you. Truth is, I've always wanted you, Serena. Since the first moment I saw you. And when I was in that cell thoughts of you kept me going. Looking back, if you hadn't come to Monaco and burst into my life again I would be dead right now. Because I was headed that way. I thought it should've been me. Not Tom. I wished I'd died instead. Until you.'

He cupped one side of her face and she nuzzled into his touch. Insanely grateful that he was still here.

'And that made me feel guilty, because suddenly I wanted to live and I thought I didn't deserve it. Then I was falling for you, and I wanted your love and I knew I'd never have it. You asked me a question that morning: why I'd waited and waited to tell you the truth, all the while digging myself into a deeper hole, until it was too late.'

She gave him a little nod.

'I was scared. Scared out of my mind. Of losing any chance I'd ever have with you. Try telling the woman you love that you were responsible for her brother's death.'

Her defences splintered as her heart swelled and beat so hard she feared it would burst from her chest. He loved her. He really loved her.

'Oh, Finn, why didn't you just tell me that? Why make out that I meant nothing to you? You hurt me.'

'I know, and I'm sorry. But I was messed up. Just wanted to push you away. Didn't believe for one second you could forgive me, let alone feel the same. The guilt and pain was crippling me, Serena. It wasn't until I read your letter. Oh, baby, your letter.' He wrapped one hand around her nape and gently kissed her forehead. 'I'm so sorry you went through that. But the more I read it the more I realised that for you to trust me with your past you had to genuinely believe Tom's death wasn't my fault. It gave me hope you had feelings for me too. And when I thought about what you went through... I've never met anyone like you. You're so beautiful and brave and strong. You make me want to fight. Be a survivor. For *you*.'

She could barely speak past the enormous lump in her throat. 'I was so worried about you. Once I realised you had some kind of survivor's guilt I thought, *I'm going to lose him too.* I would've done anything to prove that I didn't blame you.'

He frowned pensively and brushed his thumb across his bottom lip in that boyish way he did sometimes. Uneasy. As if he wanted to ask her something.

Serena laid her hands on his chest, felt his heart pound beneath her palm. 'Finn?' God, she wished she was better at this man-woman thing.

He seemed to think better of it and said, 'I owed my girl a wish, so I went to meet this shrink.'

Serena smiled up at him. She knew she was beaming but she was so proud of him.

'We do this thing…the shrink and me…where I have to come up with worse outcomes. She said it was really difficult, except I had an answer in a nanosecond.'

'What did you say?'

'*You* could have been there too. *You* could've been taken from me too.'

'Oh, Finn.'

'So I've started being grateful for that, you know?'

That was it. Moisture flooded her eyes.

'Aw, baby, I'm sorry. I keep making you cry.' Leaning down, he kissed away her tears, dusting his lips over her cheeks.

'Anything makes me cry these days. It's not natural!'

'Don't tell me. Boys don't cry, right? *Wrong*. I cried on and off for days when my mum died. Couldn't understand the injustice of it all. She was the most loving, self-sacrificing woman you'd ever meet. The good people always die.'

'That's not true. *You* didn't die, Finn, and every day I'm grateful for it.'

'You are?' he asked, with that pensive stare she couldn't quite grasp. There was something oddly endearingly vulnerable about him.

'Every day,' she assured him.

'Let it go, you said. Make a choice. Forgive myself. And I am. I'm trying. But the fact is it isn't only Tom I have regrets over. I've carried guilt for years over abandoning Eva when my mother was diagnosed. I was so selfish. Only thinking about the next race. But when I look back, the truth was I couldn't take watching her die. Seeing pain and heartbreak tear through my family again. I went to see Eva a couple weeks back, to say sorry. She doesn't blame me, Serena, not one bit. She said I had to let it go, that life was too short.'

'I like her already.'

'You'll love her. Her and Dante. They've just had a baby boy and he's amazing, and when I watched the three of them—a perfect little family—all I could think of was you and how I wanted that with you. How I could easily give up everything—the racing, the risks—to have that with you. Only you.'

She gripped the lapels of his jacket in order to stay upright. 'You want me and you to…have a family? A home? Like…together?'

He gave a somewhat sheepish shrug. 'Well, yeah, a family would be nice—but only if you want to. I'll be happy just to make you mine. Okay, you look horrified. It's too soon. I'm jumping the gun—'

'No. No. You're not. I've just never thought that far ahead before. What was the point of hoping for something I'd never have? Guess I didn't think I was wife material.'

That, she realised, had been the problem all along. Her insecurities. If she was honest she'd never been able to wrap her head around Finn wanting her. So it had been easy to think his every word and every touch was a lie. To avoid the pain of disillusionment. Heartache. So she'd run before she'd got too deep. Though in reality it had been too late. She'd already fallen.

And now—now she could have it all. And she felt like dancing and skipping and whooping and being really girly.

She bounced on her toes. 'What does a wife do, anyway?'

'She designs spectacular cars and wears biker boots and funky T-shirts. At least *my* wife will. I love you just the way you are, baby girl. You're The One for me.'

Ohh, here came the tears again. 'I am?'

'Sure you are.' He speared his fingers into her hair, rubbed the tip of her nose with his. 'I won't lie to you. I'm still scared of something happening to you. Of giving you my heart without ever holding yours in return. But if you give me a chance to prove my love, to prove that we could be good together, that I won't let you down, I can win it. I can win your heart. Just give me a chance.'

That shadowed gaze was back and she gasped, realising how intensely vulnerable he felt. 'Oh, Finn, I'm sorry. I'm such an idiot. You don't have to win it. It's yours. I'm madly, insanely in love with you.'

His head jerked so fast she reckoned he'd have whiplash in the morning. '*What?* That's impossible.'

'I promise you it is completely, utterly, absolutely possible.' She sank her fingers into the hair at his nape and pulled him down for a kiss. 'I literally fell for you when I tumbled in your window all those years ago. But you were a virtual carbon copy of my dad and I knew the rote. A boatload of broken hearts and weakened women in your wake. I hated you for making me vulnerable to that. But deep down I've always wanted you. Me all awkward and tomboyish, you all confident and sinfully beautiful—and, as it turns out, wild and honourable, with the ability to be completely and utterly selfless.'

'Hell, Serena, you scare the crap out of me when you say stuff like that. Then again, you always have.' He nuzzled into her neck. Breathed her in. 'Are you sure you…love me?'

'One billion per cent sure. Only you can make me feel like a woman. Only you can make me feel amazing. I love who I am with you. You're everything to me. I'm not saying it's going to be easy—life never is. We have millions of choices to make and sometimes we'll trip and fall and make mistakes. But we'll get through it all. We'll make it work. Together.'

Lifting his head, he ensnared her with a fierce, ardent gaze. 'You were designed especially for me—you know that? All my life I've taken risks on the track, but never with my heart. I never wanted to get close to anyone just to lose them. I didn't want to be touched—' He took her hand and laid it over his heart. 'In here. But you do more than touch me, Serena. You *own* me.'

Trust and love, hope and joy filled the warm air between them and she jumped into his arms. 'I'm yours. Take me home. Now. Please.'

With a sexy smile that made her insides gooey, he coaxed

her legs around his waist. 'That would be my place,' he said, with a hint of delicious possessiveness that promised a night to remember.

'That's what I said. I've never known what home felt like. What it was. I've been searching for it for years. Peace. Perfect blissful peace. I've finally found it, and it's in your arms.'

Finn tightened his hold and began to walk her into a future she couldn't wait to begin.

'And that's where you'll always be. Forever.'

* * * * *